"The future is fluid, Jeff.... Your situation can turn around at any time."

Jeff looked into Hope's beautiful eyes and knew the answer to his next question even before he asked it. The truth of her incredible faith in him was there in the depths of those eyes he loved so much. But there was something else there, too, and it hurt. "Do you really believe that, or is it your guilt talking?"

"I feel guilty. There's no point in denying it, but I also really believe you'll walk again."

Jeff closed his eyes. Taking a deep breath, he gazed at her again, his heart as heavy with the weight of her belief in him as his body was with his need of her. "You have more faith in me than I deserve."

Books by Kate Welsh

Love Inspired

For the Sake of Her Child #39
Never Lie to an Angel #69
A Family for Christmas #83
Small-Town Dreams #100
Their Forever Love #120
The Girl Next Door #156

*Laurel Glen

KATE WELSH

A two-time winner of Romance Writers of America's coveted Golden Heart Award and a finalist for RWA's RITA Award in 1999, Kate lives in Havertown, Pennsylvania, with her husband of thirty years. When not at work in her home-office creating stories and the characters that populate them, Kate fills her time with other creative outlets. There are few crafts she hasn't tried at least once or a sewing project that hasn't been a delicious temptation. Those ideas she can't resist grace her home or those of friends and family.

As a child she was often the "scriptwriter" in neighborhood games of make-believe. Kate turned back to storytelling when her husband challenged her to write down the stories in her head. With Jesus so much a part of her life, Kate found it natural to incorporate Him into her writing. Her goal is to entertain her readers with wholesome stories of the love between two people the Lord has brought together and to teach His truths while she entertains.

The Girl Next Door

Kate Welsh

Love Inspired®

Published by Steeple Hill Books™

STEEPLE HILL BOOKS

ISBN 0-373-87163-5

THE GIRL NEXT DOOR

Visit us at www.steeplehill.com

Printed in U.S.A.

Blessed is the man who listens to me,
Watching daily at my gates, Waiting at the posts
of my doors. For whoever finds me finds life,
And obtains favor from the LORD.

—*Proverbs* 8:34-35

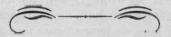

To my critique group:
These books are books of my heart
and as such are part of each of you, for each of you
holds a special place in my heart. I would not have
come so far were it not for the talents and counsel
you have all so willingly shared over the years.
Thanks for the laughter, the tears and the good
times. May we have many more to share.

Chapter One

Hope Taggert stared at her brother, wondering if during all those years Cole had been away he'd gone mad. "Why would I want to cut my hair?" she asked, thinking of the two-foot-long sable braid that lay heavily against her back. "I've always worn my hair like this."

"That's my point. It looked exactly like that when I left twelve years ago. You said you want Jeff to see you in a different light. That you don't want him thinking of you as my pain-in-the-neck little sister, Laurel Glen's trainer or—what was that you called yourself—the voice of his conscience?"

"Honestly, he has the worst taste in friends. Someone had to try to warn him," Hope said, grousing. "You don't know him the way I do anymore. We just had another argument about that crowd before he jetted off to California for this latest round of competitions."

"So there's tension between you. That's good, believe it or not." Cole's grin reminded her of days gone by. "What you need to do is something drastically different physically. Wouldn't waking him up be worth it?"

"I happen to like your sister's hair exactly as it is," Ross Taggert all but growled as he entered the sunny breakfast room.

Hope watched with dismay as the grin slid off Cole's face. Somehow when her father's penetrating voice announced his arrival, the bright and airy room became dark and stifling. And her dismay turned to anger when her father continued.

"Jeffrey Carrington isn't worthy of her time, let alone cutting her hair. And I don't want her encouraging him in that way. It's bad enough that he's around when he thinks of her as just a friend."

Hope felt her hackles rise. She loved her father. She tried to honor him at all times, as the Lord commanded. But he no longer had a right to a say in her life. Before she could form an intelligent, adult response, though, Cole picked up the usual pattern of his relationship with their father.

"You just don't want to share her," Cole challenged.

"That isn't it at all," Ross snapped. "He isn't worthy of her, and she's safer if he sees her only as an occasional friend."

"No one's good enough for your princess, isn't that it?" Cole sneered, sarcasm and irritation rife in his voice.

"She's too naive to handle a man like Carrington."

"Would you take a look at her? She isn't your little girl anymore. There's a beautiful woman hiding behind those jeans and chambray shirts. And she could do a lot worse than attracting Jeff Carrington's attention."

Ross's eyes turned frosty. "Your recommendation isn't a plus considering your track record with women, or with the rest of life for that matter."

"How would you know anything about me or my life? You haven't cared about me for years. I have a degree in veterinary medicine, but you still can't see past a few indiscretions in my adolescence. As far as you're concerned, I'm still a disgrace to the family name," Cole said.

"A few indiscretions? You were arrested for felony car theft. You didn't choose to become a solid citizen around here. Until you prove yourself to the people who knew you when, your bad record will stand with this community."

Typical, Hope thought, tuning out yet another spate of cross words. Within seconds of being in the same room, her father and brother were once again at each other's throats. Be careful what you wish for, Aunt Meg always said.

Hope had wanted her brother to come back to Laurel Glen, and now, after years away, he had. But nothing had changed. Ross and Cole's animosity toward each other hadn't faded with time as she'd hoped. Since Cole arrived home two weeks ago, being in the company of father and son was like walking through a mine field. Any subject was likely to spark an explosion. It was tiring, to say the least.

She glanced at Aunt Meg, who had lost interest in her hot cereal. The older woman's disgusted expression seemed to say, "Run for the hills. They're at it again."

Both her aunt and Hope had been through all this before. After Hope and Cole's mother was killed in a tragic accident, Aunt Meg had come back to Laurel Glen to live with them. Hope had been thirteen and Cole fifteen at the time. After Marley Taggert's death, the relationship between Ross and his son had disintegrated, and it had apparently continued along the same road in the last thirteen years since Cole left for military school at sixteen. Absence had not made their hearts grow fonder. Theirs no longer even looked like the love-hate relationship it had been back then.

Now it was all hate.

Hope stood. Cole had given her a lot to think about, and she wasn't about to get dragged into yet another argument. "Dad, since you didn't invite Jeff to the Valentine's Day party, I did," she interrupted, facing her father as he glared at Cole. "Jeff's coming as my date."

Ross's gaze swung to her. He was clearly stunned at first. "What? You know how I feel about that wastrel."

"He's *my* date. Not yours. I'm twenty-seven years old. Stop trying to pick my friends. *And* my clothes. *And* my hair style." Suddenly she didn't want to think about Cole's suggestion. She wanted to act on it and then some. "I've decided to buy a different dress than the one I wore last year. I'm going shopping."

Ross Taggert suddenly looked confused. "I helped you pick out that nice blue dress. You always look so charming in it."

"I've worn it, what…three or four years running? And that's exactly why I want a new one." She looked from her father to Cole then back. "Please don't argue all day while I'm gone." Then on impulse she turned to Cole and leaned down to kiss his cheek. "Thanks. I'll think about the hair. Who knows, maybe a whole new me will come home."

She rushed out, trying not to think about Cole's chuckle and her father's strident tone rebuking her brother as a troublemaker. Aunt Meg was in for yet another tension-filled day. Hope wanted nothing more at that moment than to knock their heads together!

It was six o'clock when Hope crept up the back stairs. She entered her room and stared at the woman—the stranger—who stared back at her from the mirror over her dresser. She looked…

Panic invaded her heart. How could she have let them cut off her hair? Even though she'd donated her hair to Locks of Love, an organization that supplied wigs to juvenile cancer patients, she'd still cut it more to spite her father than to attract Jeff.

She sighed, knowing that she'd fallen once again into the same trap Cole had lived in for years. It had been happening more and more since Ross had refused her the job as head trainer three years ago.

She'd taken a job with a competitor because her father had told her that no daughter of his was going to continue hanging around the stables with rough-and-tumble handlers for the rest of her life. To her, he'd been saying she would never be able to cut it in the job.

So she had taken the job at Lithum Creek Farm and had brought the mediocre stables up to and past the standards Ross Taggert had set for his own place. It had taken a year and a half, but one fine day Ross Taggert had come to her hat in hand. He'd begged her to leave her job and to come home. The job was hers—at an increased rate over what her current job paid. She'd agreed, but it took six months to hire and train a replacement. She'd been back home a year, and while he hadn't contradicted her in front of the men, they battled often about her decisions.

"Oh, excuse me, I was looking for Hope. Are you a friend of hers?" Hope heard Aunt Meg ask from behind.

Hope forced a smile and pivoted to face her aunt, who stood uncertainly in the doorway. "Hi, Aunt Meg."

"Oh, goodness gracious! Hope, what have you—"Oh, look at you!"

Hope's stomach rolled as she turned to do just that. She couldn't meet her aunt's eyes in the mirror. "You hate it. I look stupid, don't I? Go ahead. Tell me." Hope braced herself for the awful truth. "I saw an all-day spa and threw caution to the wind. I told them to create a whole new me. They took me at my word." She gestured to her outfit and the piles of bags on the bed. "They, uh, have a boutique. I look like I'm playing dress-up. Jeff's probably going to laugh at me."

"Laugh? My dear, you are going to knock Jeffrey Carrington's socks off! Cole certainly knew what he was talking about. You are simply gorgeous."

Hope turned quickly to face Aunt Meg and was momentarily startled by the hair that swung across her cheek before it settled into its new bouncy do. She caught her reflection in the full-length cheval mirror across the room and walked to stand in front of it.

"He was right?" Hope examined each feature of the woman in the mirror. "Cole was right," she repeated, but this time she was certain that the woman in the mirror was her—part of her that she'd always denied.

"You can never say your brother doesn't know women," Meg said sardonically.

"I was hiding, wasn't I?"

"I'd say so. Do you know why you were?" Aunt Meg asked.

"I was about to ask myself the same thing. Dad. He was so convinced a woman couldn't do my job, so I buried this part of me. I see why Cole thinks I've tried to take his place. I've been so busy trying to earn Dad's respect that I haven't been all I can be for me. I like looking like this. Dressing like this."

"Well, now, that's a start. It's okay to be beautiful, Hope. The Lord gave you your beauty."

"Mom was beautiful. Do you think Dad sees her in me? Does this hurt him?"

"I don't know what's in his heart. I wasn't here much during his marriage to your mother. And he won't talk about her even now, but I can tell you that you don't look at all like your mother. You look like my mother. Ross may have forgotten you're a woman, since you've always done work he considers traditionally male, but I don't see how he won't see it now. I'm sure he'll be proud of the lovely woman who is his daughter. And now that you see how much fun it can be, maybe I can drag you away to go shopping once in a while."

Hope grinned at her tall, willowy aunt. "I didn't get the new dress, after all. How about one night this week?"

Meg grinned in answer. "So show me all you *did* buy."

Hope got excited all over again. There was a bag full of all the things the makeup technician used to give Hope's face the look of classic beauty. She'd bought bath salts and body cream and perfume all in the same scent. She couldn't wait to soak in a nice tub instead of her usual hurried shower. According to the consultant who'd guided her through her startling remake, nothing makes you feel like a woman more than soaking in acres of bubbles and gallons of scented water. And Hope had put off womanhood long enough.

Two weeks later, Hope put the finishing touches on her makeup. Then she slipped on and buckled her new sandals. She stood in the three-inch heels then walked to the mirror and pirouetted in the middle of the floor, laughing and thinking of Jeff.

Tall and golden, Jeffrey Carrington had been the object of her love in one capacity or another from her earliest memories. Oh, sometimes when they were younger his teasing and pat-her-on-the-head mentality had pushed her to find ways to torture him as only a best friend's little sister can. But it had always been because, deep in her heart, she adored him.

A knock on her door interrupted her thoughts. "Hope, the guests are nearly all here," her father called through the door.

"Oh. Sorry. I'll be right down," she called back and checked herself one last time in the mirror. Unnecessarily, she smoothed the floor-length emerald silk sheath that she and Aunt Meg had found at a boutique, then she reached up to finger the emerald and diamond choker, a family heirloom left to Aunt Meg. She'd insisted Hope wear it the moment she'd seen Hope in the dress.

Please, Lord. Let him see me. Really see me this time.

Hope took one last deep breath and stepped into the hall. Strains of an old love song drifted up the gracefully curved stairs of the central foyer. She had just about reached the middle of the sweeping staircase when Cole opened the front door to admit a golden couple.

The man, tall and heart-stoppingly handsome,

turned toward her, and Hope gasped. Jeff had arrived. With a date. Before she could retreat, Jeff glanced up at her and stared.

Hope sought out Cole with her gaze as tears stung the back of her throat. When she found him, she mentally begged him to rescue her from her frozen stance on the stairs. She blinked away telltale moisture collecting in her eyes. She refused to cry in front of Elizabeth Boyer and Jeffrey Carrington.

Unfortunately, Jeff was two steps ahead of Cole in reaching the bottom of the stairs.

"Hope?" he said, looking at her, his voice sounding a bit odd. "You— You're—"

"I'm Hope. You got it in one, sport," she said just a tad too sharply. She took the next step and then the next till she stood gazing into his darkened gray eyes. She forced a smile, determined to brazen her way through this. "You remember me, Carrington. Bane of your existence. Oft times voice of your unused conscience. Pick your chin up off the floor. You're staring."

"And drooling," Cole growled and stepped to her side. "Come dance with me, sister mine, before everyone tries to steal you away."

Cole directed her toward the band and the nearly empty dance floor. A few years earlier the caterer had come up with an ingenious way to temporarily cover and heat the stone terraces. The candle- and moonlit dance floor was now a Valentine's Day tradition in the area. On the air was the perfume of hundreds of flowers that had been placed about the perimeter of the room, twined around the myriad candelabra and arranged in beribboned clusters that surrounded the stage.

"Are you all right?" Cole whispered.

"Other than feeling like an utter fool, you mean? I'll live. I'm tough. Hasn't Daddy told you how strong and unshakable I am?"

"Sorry to destroy the legend, but right now you're quaking like a California fault line."

"Don't let the watery eyes fool you. That's pure rage you're feeling."

"Nice try, kitten, but I saw your face when you realized he wasn't here alone."

She dropped her forehead into the hollow of Cole's shoulder. "Oh, no. Tell me he didn't see."

"No. And don't worry. He isn't leaving here tonight without the imprint of my fist somewhere on his aristocratic person."

Hope looked up, and her startled gaze locked with his. "Don't you dare! I probably wasn't clear about my invitation. I was really nervous. I shouldn't have been so vague. I should have remembered how totally dense he is about me. I don't need you to fight my battles for me. Besides, if he doesn't already know what he's done, I certainly don't want him to."

"I'll make a deal with you. You don't tell me how to be a big brother, and I won't tell you how to be a little sister. There are some perks that come with each position." He wagged his straight eyebrows at her comically, making Hope laugh aloud. "Don't spoil my fun. I've missed a lot of brothering over the years. You okay now?''

Hope nodded. ''Thanks for the rescue, big brother. I'm fine.''

''Good, because the first in a horde of men is about to sweep you away. Hi, there, Hal. You here to ask permission to horn in on my date with this beautiful creature?''

''I certainly am. Hello, Hope.''

Hope nearly groaned. Harold Pendergrass had been following her around like a puppy since junior high. Why couldn't she fall in love with him instead of a man who saw her as a sister?

What have I been thinking all these years? Jeff Carrington asked himself as he absently guided Elizabeth through the gallery toward the heated terrace where the band had set up.

He'd always insisted that Hope was the little sister his busy parents had never gotten around to providing him. And then he'd stepped inside Laurel House's foyer tonight, and his illusions had dissolved like mist in the sunshine.

As Jeff stepped through the French doors, he caught sight of Hope laughing at Cole and was relieved to see that she was only dancing with her brother. Why he felt relief he wasn't sure, and the bigger mystery was why he felt even more tense at the same time. It was the kind of tension you feel when you realize your life is about to change and you're powerless to stop it.

What he felt when he looked at Hope bore no resemblance to anything he'd feel for a sibling. His feelings were most unbrotherly and troubling.

"Am I imagining something or did something monumental just happen back there?" Elizabeth asked, dragging Jeff back from his dizzying thoughts.

Jeff shook his head and grinned. "Don't be silly."

"So Hope Taggert's new look didn't just knock you for a loop?" She grinned knowingly. "And you aren't silently thanking your lucky stars that I came here on a mission of mercy to rescue Cole from the old biddies we both know are lining up to pick him apart?"

"You're as big a pain in the neck as Hope. You know that?"

"Ah, but when I emerged from the chrysalis several years ago, you never looked at me the way you did Hope just now in the foyer."

Jeff swallowed. Had he been that obvious? "I was...surprised."

"You always were a master of understatement. She didn't look happy to see me. You did tell her I was coming along, didn't you?"

Jeff shook his head, wondering what difference it made. "Not with my flight getting canceled yesterday. I barely got in the house in time to shower and dress. Besides, Hope wants what's best for Cole, and having you at his side will make tonight easier for him. You play along, and I'll charm us into being with the right partners. Cole won't have any idea we're taking pity on him."

Jeff watched as Cole turned Hope over to Hal Pendergrass, and from the moon-eyed expression on the other man's face, his feeling for Hope hadn't changed a bit. Jeff grinned, wondering if Hope would wind up kicking her perpetual admirer in the shins the way she had in eighth grade. The grin faded when Hope smiled and slid easily into the other man's arms.

Jeff mentally catalogued the feeling that arrowed through him. Jealousy. He didn't want Hope dancing. At least not with anyone but him.

"Tell your lady friend you'll be right back. We're about to have a little talk," Cole said as he stepped up behind Jeff.

Jeff excused himself to Elizabeth and followed Cole. He hated scenes, and Cole looked annoyed. And because Cole had once been his best friend before the distance between Pennsylvania and California had thinned the bonds. They'd managed to meet up from time to time over the thirteen years since Cole left. Whenever Jeff was competing near where Cole lived, they made a point to get together, but it wasn't the same. As they turned the corner of the stone terrace, moving between one heated tent room to the next, Cole rounded on him and drove the breath out of him with a solid punch to his midsection.

"Oof." He gasped, then drew in a breath that was a great deal more painful than the previous one.

"Ouch," Cole said, shaking his hand in the air. "What are you doing, working out every day?"

"The Summer Olympics are this summer. Of

course I am. Before I return the favor, you mind telling me what that was for?''

"It was for being a dense idiot and hurting my sister. There's more where that came from if you do it again. If you don't care about her, the least you could have done was let her down easily. You didn't have to tell her how little you care by showing up with Miss Moneybags back there.''

Jeff blinked, rubbing his sore ribs. "What are you talking about?''

"Hope asked you here as *her* date, nitwit. Do you know how much trouble she's gone through for you? She even cut her hair!''

Jeff stared at Cole in horror and thought back to the phone call. In spite of feeling lower than a snake, Jeff was oddly buoyed suddenly. "She cut her hair for me?''

"Yeah. Wipe that stupid grin off your face, or have you forgotten that you showed up with a date?''

Jeff lost the grin and groaned. He'd never meant to hurt Hope. He'd not only been dense about his feelings, but hers, as well. When he'd come in and looked at her, he'd instantly wished he'd come alone. But that had been before he'd realized who the vision was who stood staring at him from above. Hope was his friend, his confidante, his touchstone. And she was lovely.

And he'd been a blind fool.

"She called me at my hotel in L.A. and asked if I'd be back in time for the party since she hadn't gotten my RSVP. I said that as far as I knew I hadn't been invited. Nothing's changed, by the way. Ross still doesn't like me. I said as much when she asked me to come tonight. She said I'd be her special guest. I swear, Cole, I had no idea she meant as her date. I don't even know what I'd have said back then if I'd realized what she was asking.''

"How about now?"

"Now I'd have been the one asking. I'm an idiot. No wonder I haven't been able to find the woman for me. I couldn't see the forest for the trees. She's been right in front of me all along."

"And when did you have this great epiphany?" Cole asked.

Jeff heard Cole's skepticism. "When I looked up and I realized my best friend and baby sister wasn't my sister at all."

"Then it might be a good idea if you asked her to dance *before* you dance with—what's her name?"

"Her name is Elizabeth Boyer. She's Reggie Boyer's daughter. You know, my coach. Don't you remember her?"

Cole frowned, and Jeff knew a mental image of Elizabeth as his friend had last seen her must have sharpened in Cole's mind. "The pudgy carrottop with the freckles and teeth? No way."

"Yes, way."

"She was a sixteen-year-old boy's worst nightmare." Cole searched out the woman in question. "And she's every twenty-nine-year-old's fantasy."

"Then you'd be interested in keeping her company? In fact, why not take over for me tonight? I'll tell Hope I brought her along for you and that you both misunderstood my intentions.''

Cole nodded. ''I think I could make the sacrifice for my sister. But what about Elizabeth? I've hurt enough women in the last few years. Her heart isn't engaged, is it?''

Jeff shook his head. As she said earlier, he'd never seen her as more than his coach's daughter. But he couldn't tell Cole the truth of why he'd brought Elizabeth. He had to be more subtle than that. If Cole had one failing it was that he had too much pride. ''We're just friends. Her father's my coach, remember? Explain to her what's going on and she'll understand.''

Cole arched an eyebrow and grinned. ''I'll consider that your blessing, in that case.'' Then the smile faded and his eyes turned cold. ''Hurt my sister again, Carrington, and you'll wish you'd never been born.''

He'd never seen Cole more deadly serious. ''You don't have to worry,'' Jeff assured him, and turned away. Just then, he caught sight of Hope whirling in someone's arms and his thoughts turned back to her and the evening ahead. He knew he was grinning like an idiot and he didn't care who saw.

She'd cut her hair for him.

Chapter Two

Jeff stopped short. Hope was dancing with Ross Taggert. If he asked her now, Ross might cause a scene and embarrass both him and Hope.

"If you're going to let my father stop you, you may as well collect Elizabeth now and step out of my sister's life," Cole murmured from behind him.

"He hates me, and I've never known why."

"I think you remind him of my mother's social set, and he wants to keep you away from his precious little girl."

"That can't be right. Your father adored your mother. Everyone knows how he still grieves for her."

"You think so?" Cole snapped. "Believe me, appearances can be deceiving. The song's just about over. Go on. Go claim your date. Think of it as really getting his goat if it helps."

Jeff turned to Cole. When they'd talked last, Hope

had said the bitterness between Cole and Ross was even worse. It was sad, but Jeff understood more than most. His relationship with his own late father hadn't been the best.

"I'll try not to hurt Hope, Cole, but don't you hurt her, either. You have no idea how responsible she's always felt for the rift between you and Ross. Stop using her. You did it before, and you're still doing it now. So is your father."

Leaving Cole gaping, Jeff pivoted and approached Hope and Ross. They stepped away from each other as the song ended, but Ross kept hold of her hand.

"I hate to admit it, but Cole was right about cutting your hair. You're beautiful. I never realized how much you look like my mother," Ross was saying as Jeff stepped next to him.

"For once we agree on something, Ross," Jeff said. Though he spoke to the father, Jeff's couldn't take his eyes off the daughter. "She certainly is a beautiful woman. I was hoping I could have the next dance. There's a misunderstanding we need to clear up."

Hope smiled but, in her bottomless blue eyes, Jeff saw how deep a hurt he'd caused her.

"What about Elizabeth?" she asked. "You haven't even danced with her."

So she'd noticed. "Elizabeth *is* the misunderstanding," he told Hope, taking her hand. He turned her away from her father and into his arms, where Jeff was beginning to believe she just might belong. Now that she stood in his embrace, he wondered why he'd never noticed the way her nearness affected him. The only time he was ever truly happy when he was with her, he realized. And even Cole hadn't been as good a friend as she was. There was almost nothing he could not or would not share with her. He felt a helpless grin tip his lips up at the corners. He even loved arguing with her. Her mind was quick, her heart fierce and her spirit pure. And he vowed at that moment that she would be his.

"What's this about a misunderstanding?" Hope asked.

Her question yanked him out of his thoughts. "Oh. Elizabeth is Cole's date, not mine. I thought it might make tonight easier for him if he had a lovely woman on his arm. One who's also well accepted in the community. When he left, he wasn't high on everyone's list."

Hope blinked, then gave Jeff a sad smile. "I never thought of you as dishonest. It's always been one of your more redeeming qualities."

Jeff winced. "I'm sorry. That was a half truth. I also misunderstood your invitation," he admitted. "But I really did bring her for Cole. When she came to L.A. to visit her father last week, we got to talking about tonight and Cole. It really will be better for him if Elizabeth is with him. This community isn't going to let him off the hook too easily." Jeff hesitated and grinned at Hope. It was something that had been getting him out of hot water with women since he noticed they were a different gender. He only wished he knew why. "You aren't going to desert me now that I gave away my dance partner, are you?"

Hope arched one of her delicately defined eyebrows, as if to say, Haven't you learned not to try that with me yet? She said, "I'll think about it."

Jeff felt an unfamiliar jolt. "You don't believe me."

"Take it or leave it, Carrington."

Jeff forced himself to relax. It would be fine. He would just have to charm her into forgiving him. Piece of cake. Undaunted, he grinned at Hope. "Then I guess the night's mine."

But when she brought her gaze to his, with a knowing look in her eyes, he realized two things. He was probably in love, and if he was then he was in big trouble. Hope was one tough cookie under the soft new look, and nothing where she was concerned would ever be a piece of cake.

The flowers arrived just as Hope and Aunt Meg came downstairs on their way to church the next morning. "Where on earth did he find a florist to deliver on a Sunday?" Aunt Meg asked as Hope closed the door after the delivery boy.

"He who? We don't even know who they're from. They could be from Harold Pendergrass."

Aunt Meg arched one thin eyebrow. "My dear, I know a besotted fool from a besotted man. Those are from Jeffrey, believe me."

Hope opened the card and chuckled at the inscription.

"Don't torture your auntie this early in the morning. Read it. Unless it's too personal, that is."

"It isn't all that personal. Just a little embarrassing. 'Sorry we got our wires crossed. Thanks for a wonderful night. Lunkhead Carrington.'"

"See, I told you. What kind of flowers? Come on. Open. Open," Aunt Meg urged.

Hope untied the satin ribbon to uncover a dozen white roses. "Oh. They're so delicate," Hope whispered, carefully touching the fragrant blooms.

"*And* out of the ordinary. Harold would have done red and sent them tomorrow. You see the difference? I think you picked a winner."

"Last night Jeff took pity on two very hard up friends."

"Let me tell you, the look on Jeffrey Carrington's face when he looked at you all night had nothing to do with pity and everything to do with possession. Didn't you notice an immediate lack of dance partners after he whisked you away from your father, when before that there was a steady stream of them?"

"Well, yes." Hope smiled. "You think he really wanted to be with me, after all?"

Aunt Meg took the flowers and handed Hope her coat, then she gave the roses to the housekeeper, who crossed the foyer at that moment. "Sally, please put these in that Waterford vase I picked up at auction last month, then put them in Hope's room."

"Good idea," Hope said. "That way Daddy won't see them. May as well avoid one argument." She sighed. "Remember when it was quiet and peaceful around here?"

Aunt Meg stared at her for a long moment. "Not since you set your sights on Howard Sothsbie's position when he was approaching retirement. Cole's livened things up more than is comfortable, but peaceful? Before? You should be on the sidelines." She flipped her cape over her shoulders in a typical dramatic Meg Taggert move. "We're off to church now, Sally dear. Thank you for taking care of the flowers." She turned and strode through the front door, her cape flying in the winter breeze.

Hope shrugged and followed her aunt outside. She finally caught up with the fifty-year-old dynamo as Meg slid behind the wheel of her silver BMW.

"We need to have a chat, my darling," Aunt Meg said as she turned the key in the ignition, then put the car in gear. "I sent those flowers to your room so you would have them to dream on. You cannot retreat to the old Hope. You took a stand with Ross and you have to hold your ground."

"You make this sound like a battle."

Meg grinned. "It is. As you learned when you quit Laurel Glen and started working for Lithum Creek Farm, peace at any price isn't worth it."

Hope turned in her seat to face Meg. "But there's so much tension already right now. You're getting a case of indigestion with every meal."

Meg chuckled, her marvelous voice dipping low. She sometimes reminded Hope of a Christian Auntie Mame. "Let me worry about my digestion. I could stand to lose a few pounds. I'll let it be known when I've had enough. My point is…well, look at this thing between Cole and Ross. Yes, it has been relatively peaceful around here these past thirteen years but the bitterness between them has gone way beyond where it was when Cole left to finish high school at sixteen. You see? Our peace wasn't worth the price of the hatred they show each other now."

"You're saying by avoiding a clash over Jeff now, it could make it worse later. But I'm still not even sure there will be a later. He could very well have been being kind."

"Let me tell you about men staking out their territory when a woman catches their eye. It's an unmistakable expression that few men miss when it's aimed at them. And your Jeff wore it all night after he claimed that first dance. Are you going to hide your relationship from Ross?"

"I don't want to, but I don't want to cause more friction right now. You saw him shooting daggers at Jeff all night. Can you imagine the arguments Cole and Dad will get into if I toss another thing for them to disagree about into the mix? You saw what my stupid haircut caused."

"I understand, but if you start sneaking around, Jeff will soon see that he isn't first in your heart. He's never been first with anyone in his whole life but Emily Roberts, and she's been on the payroll since before he was born. You have the power to change that young man's life and touch his soul. Use that power carefully. And don't make this too easy on him. A little groveling will be just as good for his soul. He has to work to get you.''

Meg flipped down the vanity mirror in front of Hope and tapped it to draw her attention to the new woman reflected there. It still surprised Hope after two weeks when she caught sight of herself in a mirror.

''And the reason he has to work to get you is that you, my dear, are a prize worthy of a bit of questing!''

Friday dawned as one of those rare February days that teases the senses with its promise of spring. It was a warm sunny fifty-five degrees, and since there'd been little rain or snow, the fields weren't muddy. It was the perfect day for a ride, which was only one of the reasons Hope was so elated.

Jeff had once again sent flowers and had once again apologized for their mix-up. He'd called every day to ask her to do something with him. Taking Meg's advice, she'd made excuses that she knew he was bright enough to figure out were just that. But this time he'd begged her to go riding with him. He'd sounded desperate, and she couldn't hold out the full week Meg had suggested. She'd invited him to come over to ride with her. He'd agreed in a heartbeat but had sounded surprised that she invited him to come there. Meg was apparently right about letting Jeff know she'd stand up to her father over him.

A shoo-in for the United States Olympic Equestrian team and a possible gold medalist, Jeff had already ridden his mount early that morning in the practice ring, so he'd agreed to ride one of Laurel Glen's mounts that needed exercise. She had both horses saddled and ready to go by the time she saw the roof of Jeff's black four-by-four gleaming in the sun as it moved quickly along the drive toward the stables.

Dressed in tan riding pants and a hunter green jacket, he jumped out of the four-by-four and reached in for his riding helmet. Hope felt at ease in the riding outfit Meg had found for her. For once she wasn't hideously underdressed in jeans and an old tweed blazer. Jeff, his eyes sparkling in the sunlight, didn't comment on the change in her normal dress.

"What a day!" he called to her.

Hope jumped off the fence where she'd perched to wait for him, trying to look casual but feeling anything but.

"I know it's just an aberration but I swear there's spring in the air," she said, praying she sounded as if this were just a day like any other.

"So, who did you give me?" he asked as she fell in step next to him.

As they made their way toward the stone stables and the paddock where she'd left the saddled horses, he settled his arm across her shoulders and tucked her against his side. Hope felt her heart pick up its already too quick beat. She knew in that moment that this was anything but just another ride with a friend. It was the beginning of something wonderful.

"Golden Boy or Ross's Prize," she answered around the lump in her throat.

Jeff stopped in his tracks, then stepped in front of

her, taking her shoulders in his strong, gentle hands. Her heart was pounding by the time she gathered her composure enough to look into his silvery eyes. They were narrowed and grave as he spoke. "Hope, your father would have a fit if I rode Prize, and you know it."

"He said both of them needed exercise. Which one would you rather ride?"

"Prize," Jeff admitted and grinned, however reluctantly.

She took his hand and pulled him along, and a carefree excitement seemed to shimmer in the air. "Then let's mount up and get at it. We're wasting the warmth of the day. This weather won't last long."

They were on their way in seconds, and Hope lost most of her nervousness. This was Jeff. Her pal. Her friend. His laughter rang out as they put the horses through their paces, taking fences and hedgerows and riding rings around each other.

Hope made it a practice to sit back and watch him ride. He thought she was helping him perfect his form, but often she just watched the beauty of him in motion, so attuned to his mount—even a strange one—that they moved as one. She pulled Golden Boy to a halt at the top of a hill that afforded a view of both Laurel Glen and Lavender Hill, Jeff's estate and breeding farm.

He and Prize took the last hedge and charged up the hill after her. "How was that?" he called on his way up.

"Perfect. You're really ready this time."

"I hope so. I don't know if I want to be doing this in another four years."

Hope nodded and looked around. "I love this view. Have you thought any more about getting Lavender Hill up and running again as a full-service farm?"

Jeff's smile turned sad. "You mean other than that Father and Mother are already spinning in their graves because I'm breeding stock?"

"How long are you going to go on trying to please them? You went to the college you did because it was what they expected. You joined that stupid snooty fraternity because it was the right one to join. Sometimes I think the only reason you're working so hard for the Olympics is that it gives you a blue-blooded excuse to ride. They're gone, Jeff. You don't have to win their notice by living your life in their *right way* any more."

Jeff narrowed his gray eyes beneath the velvet peak of his helmet. "Well, you're back at home again."

Hope nodded. "But I made Dad come after me and beg me to come back. And he had to give me a raise. I've always been faithful to the Lord, much to my father's annoyance. And I did invite you to the Valentine's Party." She grinned. "And you're on his favorite horse right now."

"Prize is incredible, by the way. I wish Ross had sold him to me. I'd be a shoo-in at the trials with him."

"You're a shoo-in anyway. Mr. March is a wonderfully trained animal."

Jeff grimaced comically. "I still can't believe I let you talk me into naming him that."

Hope laughed. "It'll keep you humble when you're on the podium wearing that gold medal. They'll be playing the national anthem and you'll be thinking about how to explain his name to the reporters."

Jeff stared at her, suddenly serious. "Why am I riding Ross's Prize, Hope?"

Hope knew what he was asking. Her heart pounded. Jeff had always wanted a chance to ride Prize, and saddling him had been a conscious decision on her part. The answer he sought was a telling one. She took a deep breath and plunged ahead. "Because this was a good way to show my father who I'd choose if I'm forced to make a choice between you and him. Considering your parents, I thought maybe you needed to know that."

"I did need to know that because—" he began, but Hope was suddenly nervous. If Jeff felt as she did, their relationship would change forever and there would be no going back. She wheeled Golden Boy away and downhill.

Hope would never know what Jeff had intended to say. As he followed her over the first hedge, the world went instantly insane. She watched it happen as if it were in slow motion while recognizing that time was moving full speed ahead. Prize left the ground with Jeff in perfect position, but then, in the next split second, the saddle broke loose and Jeff was falling backward. A look of surprise and consternation crossed his features, but that quickly changed. He landed on his back on the hard-packed soil, and his face contorted in pain. Then he went slack and still.

Hope was at his side without remembering her dismount or falling to her knees. "Jeff!" she shouted, but he didn't respond. She looked toward the cluster of buildings half a mile away then at him lying broken on the ground. She had no choice but to leave him there. He needed help. And he needed it now.

Ross's Prize had bolted as soon as Jeff hit the ground, but he wasn't headed for the stables, so no one would know there was a problem. Harry Donovan was about to mount up when Hope galloped into the main yard. There were several other workers standing around "Call nine-one-one," she shouted to no one in particular. "Jeff was thrown. He's unconscious. Send the ambulance to the first rise above the eastern paddocks."

The farm foreman frowned as he pulled out a cell phone. "You let Jeffrey Carrington ride Ross's Prize?"

"And he's running loose. I have to get back to Jeff." Hope wheeled away and thundered up the hill, Donovan bringing up the rear. She didn't want Jeff coming to alone and trying to get up. It would be up to the paramedics to say if it was safe for him to move.

But that didn't turn out to be a problem, because he didn't come to at all. Not when the paramedics arrived, sirens screaming. Not when they carefully rolled him so they could strap him to a back board. Not when they called for the rescue helicopter, nor by the time it took off, leaving her to watch him fly off alone in the care of strangers.

His whole life, Jeff had been alone.

No one was up at Laurel House, so Hope left a message with Sally and drove to the hospital. Later she would realize that she didn't remember starting the car, or leaving Laurel Glen, or running into the emergency ward. The first thing she recalled was making a call to her church's prayer chain after being told Jeff was still unconscious. She asked the chain leader to find someone to go break the news and to stay with Mrs. Roberts, Lavender Hill's longtime housekeeper and the only real mother Jeff had ever known.

Then Hope had time to think. And to place blame. And that blame was all hers. When the paramedics had arrived, she'd picked up the saddle to get it out of their way and had been appalled by the condition of the girth. She'd stared in horror at the cracked and broken leather and the buckles still attached to the saddle. How, she asked herself over and over, had she missed such a danger when she'd saddled Prize for Jeff?

She paced and paced, going over and over that morning in her mind. But she'd been so excited by the flowers and his eagerness to ride with her. And nervous. She'd been keyed up and distracted. Had she been so distracted that she hadn't obeyed safety rules? How could she have let herself forget to check the condition of the tack?

She just didn't know.

At some point, Hope realized she had her fist so tightly clenched that her nails had scraped her palm raw. She went to wash her hands, fully aware of the danger of abrasions when working around animals. The burning sensation subsided some, but that left her with only her fears for Jeff and her guilt to haunt and consume her once again.

She found herself at a bank of windows staring at the sky. *Lord, please watch over Jeff and keep him safe. I love him. I know You would rather I love another believer, but that isn't going to happen. I've tried to put my feelings for him aside, but I guess I've loved Jeff too long to stop. My dream has always been to show him Your salvation, but I can't do that if You let him die. Please give him back to me.*

"Hope?" Cole called as he strode into the waiting room. "What happened?" he asked as he gathered her in his arms. "Manuel said Jeff fell off Prize. That's ridiculous. Jeff rides like he's glued to the saddle."

"The saddle came off and Jeff with it. I still can't believe it. We were up on the rise between the two properties standing still and talking. Then we rode downhill, and when he took the first hedgerow, Jeff was suddenly flying backward and so was the saddle. He hit hard and he's been out since, as far as I know. They won't tell me anything because I'm not family. But Cole, he hasn't got any family, and I need to know. Someone should be with him."

Cole squeezed her shoulders. "Sit down and try to relax. I'll see what I can do."

* * *

Cole sauntered up to the young nurse at the desk and leaned on the tall counter, curling his ringless left hand over the edge about two feet in front of her face. "Hi, there. I wonder if you could help me." He beamed his best lady-killer smile at her.

She sent back what he was sure was her best come-hither grin and leaned a bit forward trying to show off her considerable cleavage. Cole was immune to the whole dating game, but she couldn't know that.

"I can sure try." She all but purred the words. "What can I do for you?"

"I understand you have Jeffrey Carrington here. I'd like a report on his condition. I'm Dr. Cole Taggert."

He could have sworn dollar signs flashed in her eyes. "Certainly, Doctor. Meet me at those double doors. I'll let you in."

Cole turned and winked at Hope, then approached the doors behind which he was sure Jeff was being treated. They swung open, and he followed the nurse to a big central desk where an Asian man in a lab coat and scrubs scribbled in an illegible script in a steel chart.

"Dr. Chin, this is Dr. Cole Taggert," the nurse said. "He's here about Mr. Carrington. Dr. Taggert, this is Dr. Chin, chief of neurology here at Paoli Memorial."

The man stood and stretched out his hand. "Pleasure to meet you, Doctor."

Nothing like a little professional courtesy, Cole thought as he accepted the chart. He'd never understand why medical doctors couldn't master simple penmanship. He'd have been drummed out of veterinary school for handwriting like this. He handed it back. "Uh, I'm afraid I flunked illegible scrawl one-oh-one. Could you catch me up on my friend's condition? He has no family but is about to become engaged to my sister."

"Ah. This is personal for you, then. All right. We've ruled out brain injury. He was conscious for a while but we had to sedate him rather heavily when he became agitated over his condition. From what I can see from my exam and the MRI, there is some compression of the spinal cord at L-five S-one, which has produced paralysis, loss of some feeling and weakness of the lower extremities."

Cole was instantly glad he hadn't pretended to be Jeff's doctor. He'd never have been able to hide his reaction. He could feel the blood drain from his head. "He's paralyzed?"

Chin pursed his lips, then nodded and went on clinically describing what in effect was the end of all Jeff's Olympic dreams and then some. "As you know, there have been considerable breakthroughs in the treatment of spinal cord injury. His condition could improve quickly or with time and work, but he didn't seem to hear me say that. What function he has in six months will tell us how well he'll recover. We've given him a corticosteroid to reduce the swelling and minimize further damage."

"So we wait and see?"

Dr. Chin frowned. "He'll need extensive therapy, of course."

"I'd appreciate it if my sister could be with him. As I said, Jeff's all alone but for her and his staff. Also it might help to realize that until today Jeff was a shoo-in for not only a spot on the U.S. Olympic Equestrian team but for a gold medal, as well."

Chin nodded. "I can understand why he was so devastated. I'll see that your sister has liberal access to him. He'll be sent upstairs at any minute to the fourth floor. Room four-oh-eight. You might want to take your sister up there to wait for him." The doctor smiled. "So what is your speciality, or are you in general practice?"

Cole grimaced. Granny Taggert's training was inconvenient at the worst times. "My speciality? Equine surgery, actually. I'd better get back to my sister. Thanks for your help."

The doctor's soft laughter didn't lighten Cole's heart in the least as he made his way to the automatic doors at the end of the corridor. This wasn't going to be easy. He didn't know where he'd find the words to destroy Hope's world.

She ran toward him when he exited the treatment area. "How is he?"

"Come on. Let's sit down." Cole took her by the arm and directed her to a chair in the waiting room. She sank bonelessly into it and looked at him, her blue eyes awash with tears.

"He's dead, isn't he?"

Cole squatted and took her hands. "No, kitten, but he's got some big problems."

Her voice shook. "What kind of problems?"

There was no easy way to say it. "He's paralyzed."

"No. Oh, no. I can't believe I did this to him. It's all my fault. I invited him. I missed the damaged girth."

"Don't, Hope. It could just as easily have been a car accident."

"But it wasn't."

Cole's cell phone rang and he reached for it. "Hold on a second, kitten. This is from Laurel Glen." He pushed the talk button. "Hello?"

"It's me," his father said. "Where are you and what's all this about that boneheaded Carrington riding Prize and getting dumped off? Some Olympic contender."

Cole gritted his teeth. "I'm with Hope at the hospital. Jeff's not good. It looks as if he's paralyzed. We don't know how permanent that is yet." Cole's eyes widened at his father's language. "Dad!"

"Sorry. Tell Hope I'm sorry he was hurt."

That didn't sound as if he intended to come to the hospital. Cole looked at Hope, who sat staring ahead, tears rolling down her cheeks. She needed her father, not a brother who'd been gone for thirteen years. "What time do you expect to get here?"

"I don't," Ross Taggert snapped. "Something's wrong with Prize and I need you to look at him. He's hurt and in considerable pain."

"It's probably because he was balanced for a hundred and ninety pounds of rider and tack that suddenly went airborne before he landed. I hate to leave Hope here alone."

"Well, don't expect me to go there," Ross Taggert snapped. "If she hadn't let him ride my horse without my permission, none of this would have happened."

Cole gripped the phone tighter, annoyed by his father's attitude and worried about Hope and Jeff. He felt torn. "I'll come home, but I'm heading back here as soon as I get a look at Prize." He disconnected, not waiting for a reply, and hunkered down in front of Hope. "Listen, when they found Prize, he was hurt. I'll be back as soon as I get a look at him and take care of whatever's wrong."

"Isn't Daddy coming?" Hope asked Cole as he clipped the cell phone to his belt.

Cole glanced at his watch. "Uh, no. He said he's sorry Jeff's hurt."

"He's not sorry. He hates Jeff. I'd like you to give him a message for me. Tell him what I told Jeff earlier today. If Dad forces me to choose between him and Jeff, Dad loses."

Chapter Three

The first thing Jeff saw when the fog in his brain lifted was Hope's lovely face. She was staring at him as if trying to will him awake. He was glad to grant her wish. "Hi, there," he said, then frowned. Why did he sound so woozy?

"Hi, yourself. You gave us all a terrible scare. But it's all going to be fine now. We'll get you well."

He remembered then. He'd been about to tell Hope how he felt about her when she'd gotten all skittish and taken Golden Boy downhill. He'd followed, but then during a perfectly routine jump, the world had dropped out from beneath him. He didn't even remember hitting the ground. Just a feeling of dizziness as he slid backward when he should have been flying over the jump on Prize's back.

And he remembered Hope screaming his name.

How, he wondered, could life change so drastically

in a few seconds? His life was gone—over. He might as well be dead.

"What happened?" he asked, nearly desperate to hear it confirmed by the person who'd shared so life-ending an event.

"Prize took the hedge and the saddle broke away. I can't remember it being at all damaged when I tightened the girth." Hope bit her lip, clearly fighting tears. "I'm so sorry," she whispered brokenly.

He wanted to tell her not to feel responsible. That accidents happened. He wanted to tell her to go home and get on with her life, but his eyes grew heavy again, and soon he was floating away from her to a place where he could still fly over the fields and laugh with her as they rode.

Jeff opened his eyes some time later and stared at the green ceiling. Who on earth had had the poor taste to paint a bedroom institutional green? The clatter of a cart drew his attention and he watched, detached from his body, as a young woman walked to his bed. Without ceremony she stuck a needle in an IV tube.

He frowned, remembering. He was in the hospital. In some sort of weird bed with rings at the bottom and top attached to some sort of framework that surrounded him. He couldn't move his legs, and some fool had kept him alive. "Too much," he told the nurse, though his lips and tongue felt numb.

"This is just a muscle relaxer to keep your back from going into spasms again. Don't worry. It won't hurt you and it shouldn't knock you out."

"No. You don't get it. Give me too much. Kill me. Got it?"

He heard a gasp from the foot of the bed and found Hope staring at him in horror. His heart constricted. She was still there. She'd heard.

He'd drag her down with him. His life was clearly over, and he couldn't stand to let this thing destroy Hope the way it had him.

"Go away, Hope. There's no need for you to sit there and watch me lying here. From what Dr. Chin said, this is about as exciting as I'm ever going to get."

"Of course, it isn't."

Hope hurried to his side and took his hand. He wanted to feel her touch into eternity. It was such a temptation to tie her to him, but he couldn't do that to the free spirit that was Hope. She'd been crying. It was blatantly obvious. He hated the thought of her tears almost as much as the forced smile she tried to hide them with.

"And you say *I'm* a poor liar," he challenged.

"I'm serious. You're going to be out of that bed in no time. There's no way yet to know how much you'll improve when the swelling decreases. I'm not leaving you. And Cole was here earlier, too, but there was some sort of emergency at home. He'll be back as soon as he can get here."

"Tell him not to bother. He has better things to do than waste his time on me."

"Don't be silly. Cole is your friend. Where else

would he be when you need him? Where else would *I* be?"

"I'd prefer you be anywhere else." Remembering how badly he'd done at lying to her on Saturday night, he turned his head. "Look, Hope, when the horse reared, I was about to tell you that you were barking up the wrong tree with your feelings for me. You're the little sister I never had. And a friend. But you'll never be more. I shouldn't have led you on at the Valentine's dance. But handing Elizabeth off to Cole was too big a break to pass up. I was doing him a favor getting them together, but Cole wouldn't have appreciated the gesture. Telling Cole I wanted to spend time with you was a good way not to give Elizabeth's intentions away."

"Oh."

The hollow hurt in her voice nearly killed him, but he had to let it stand. He had to make her get out of there. But before he could go further, Cole stepped into the doorway. He looked as bad as Hope.

"How's it going, buddy?" Cole asked, quietly.

Jeff responded in what was undoubtedly the least chivalrous comment he'd ever made in front of a lady in his entire life.

"That's pretty bad," Cole said lightly, clearly trying to lessen the impact of the ugly phrase, but then he sobered. "I got back here as soon as I could."

"That's good. You can get Hope to leave. I told her not to blame herself. Accidents happen."

Cole shook his head. "I don't think she's about to desert a friend like that."

Hope. He knew her. She'd stay glued to his side whether he ever got out of this crazy contraption of a bed again or not. She was blaming herself. Jeff looked from Cole to Hope. There was one way to make sure he didn't drag Hope down with him. "I'm not up to company of any kind." He studiously ignored her hurt and confusion. This was for the best. "I don't want you back here again. Leave me alone."

"Jeff?" Hope's voice sounded small and wounded. "It isn't hopeless."

He gritted his teeth. That's exactly what his life was about to become. "If we were ever friends, we aren't anymore. You're smothering me, and there's nothing I hate more. Get out, Hope." Jeff turned his head away, and when he looked back minutes later, he was alone.

Now he could let his tears fall. Now he really *had* lost everything. Now he'd lost his Hope.

Two weeks later, time hadn't improved his paralysis and the doctors continued to lie, saying he could still see improvement at any time. They sent therapists and more doctors. But he knew it was hopeless.

Just like his life. Hopeless.

He'd banned Hope from his room. He wasn't proud of hurting her, but he knew it was for her own good, and he even thought Cole more or less understood that he couldn't let her sacrifice even an hour on him.

In the past two weeks, he'd lost all dignity. He was grateful his parents hadn't lived to see this. There'd been no room in their lives for imperfection, and he was about as imperfect as you could get. They would have been appalled by his helpless condition.

He was appalled.

He was going home today, but the doctors wanted him to go to some sort of rehabilitation facility. Jeff just wanted to go home and hide where no one could see him. He'd had it with visitors.

In the last two weeks they'd arrived as a steady flow at first and had thankfully dwindled to an annoying few. Either they treated him with an embarrassing kind of pity, asked humiliating questions about how much of his body still functioned or shot subtle little barbs at him about his lack of mobility. These were the people he'd considered friends, but Hope had been telling him for years they were no more than opportunists and social climbers.

He'd always known she was right, but he'd never needed anyone before, so it hadn't mattered. They'd filled his idle time, and he'd thought they would again. But now, when it did matter, he had no one. Which, he told himself, was just as well.

He wanted to crawl into a hole and pull it in after him. But he couldn't even crawl anymore.

"I'm sorry you feel that way, Mrs. Larchmont. Butternut and Stephanie are working well together," Hope told the pushy mother. Then listened as the woman, who didn't know which end of a horse to feed, told Hope that her Steffie needed an animal with spirit and that as her parents it was their duty to see she had what she needed. The couple had bought the perfect stallion that morning, and he would be arriving any day. Butternut was up for sale.

"Fine, we'll await his arrival and see how well Stephanie takes to him. See you Tuesday." Hope dropped the phone in the cradle and buried her face in her hands.

Lord give me strength.

Another nitwit. In the four weeks since Jeff's accident, they'd lost more than fifty percent of their business due to rumors of carelessness at Laurel Glen. Now Mildred Larchmont was insisting her ninety-pound skittish child could control a stallion named Demon.

Hope dropped her hands, flipped her month-at-a-glance calendar back a page and stared at the twenty-first of February. One month ago to the day. The date of Jeff's accident sat there in its little box unmarked, unchecked. She needed no reminder. She'd never forget that date if she lived to be a thousand. It was the day she'd lost not only her best friend but the love of her life, as well.

A month. She couldn't remember a month in her whole life when she hadn't seen Jeff at least once if he was in town. But he wouldn't see her. Two years older than Cole, Jeff had always been in her life because their mothers were friends. The boys had played together since Cole was a toddler. So Jeff had been around from her earliest memory. He used to tell her she'd pulled his hair from her crib and she was still yanking his chain.

And now Jeff had summarily cut her from his life.

He'd gone so far as to have a guard put on the gate to turn her away. Her brother went to see him several times a week, but he always shook his head when he returned. Jeff still refused to see her.

She was nearly positive that he'd lied about his feelings for her. Jeff didn't have a cruel bone in his body, and it would have been cruel to send her flowers, beg to see her, stroll along the drive with his arm around her and then plan to tell her she was nothing more than a substitute for the sister he'd never had. Either he blamed her for what had happened even though he'd said he didn't or he was trying to save her from his daily struggle.

Whatever his reasons, guilt weighed on her. He was alone and hurt because of her, no matter how she looked at the situation. She prayed about it, and for Jeff, but nothing had changed. She still had to rely on progress reports from Emily Roberts when she saw Lavender Hill's housekeeper on Sundays and Wednesdays at church and on what Cole told her, which was very little. Emily's reports, however, were so depressing that Hope understood Cole's reluctance to go into detail.

From what Emily said, Jeff wasn't trying to get better. Cole said the doctor in the E.R. mentioned that Jeff had a six-month window of opportunity to regain full use of his legs. But Emily said he'd fired everyone who'd tried to push him toward exercise and therapy. Hope stared at the date. March twenty-first. One sixth of his time was gone.

Hope looked up when her father walked into the

office. Relations between them were better, but Hope knew it had nothing to do with any attitude adjustment on his part. Any improvement was due to the absence of Jeff from her life and her own determination to forgive her father's lack of support the day of the accident. She prayed daily to feel the forgiveness she'd decided to grant.

"Sorry, Daddy. Mrs. Larchmont won't budge. Want to buy Butternut? A stallion named Demon arrives before Tuesday. I hope that child doesn't get hurt. I don't know what else to do."

"See if Cole gets any bad vibes before you put her up on the stallion."

His sarcasm wasn't lost on Hope. She slapped her hand on her scarred oak desk. "That crack was unnecessary. Cole really does have an incredible rapport with the horses."

"I don't know Cole anymore, but that's what I hear."

"You know, if you'd stop trying to find fault with him all the time, and if you'd stop baiting him, maybe you would know him. He came home to try working things out with you. If you look, you might find out what a wonderful man your son really is."

"He has an attitude with me that just sets my teeth on edge. Always has."

"Always, Daddy? Or just since Mother was killed?" Hope asked. She saw the anger leap in his eyes, but she pushed on. Living and working at Laurel Glen had become intolerable, and things had to change. Aunt Meg was right. How long were they going to tiptoe around the tragedy that had split their family?

"And your point is?" he asked, suddenly tight-lipped and tense, his hands fisted on his jeans-clad hips.

"My point is that you two have to work through Mother's death or neither of you will ever get past your grief. It keeps you both mired in the past. You have to admit that maybe he did sense something in the horse that day. And he has to admit that you made a mistake. An honest one. You have to accept it, too."

Hope's heart softened. She knew how much it hurt to love as deeply as her father had only to lose that love. "When she died, all this started. She wouldn't have wanted to come between the two of you."

"You don't know—" Her father stopped short and frowned. Then he nodded stiffly. "I'll try if he will."

"He *is* trying. He came home. Imagine how hard that had to be for him. He left here in disgrace. Military school or juvenile hall. Some choice. He's a respected man away from here. Don't rise to the bait if he baits you. Don't bait him or criticize every word that comes out of his mouth. Don't question his judgment where the stock is concerned. He's the one with the degree, remember?"

Ross smiled. "I guess we're driving you and your aunt crazy."

"You guess? Aunt Meg has a permanent case of indigestion. You two have ruined every meal we've tried to eat as a family in the eight weeks he's been back."

The phone rang, and Hope said a quick prayer that it wasn't another customer canceling lessons or making plans to retrieve a horse. Rumors of a poor safety record were deadly in their world.

It wasn't. It was Emily Roberts, Jeff's housekeeper. "Hope, you have to come over here," she said without preamble. "I'm at my wits' end with him and this place."

Hope looked up. Her father looked at her expectantly. She covered the mouthpiece. "It's personal— not a customer. Why don't you go on up to the house for lunch? And could you tell Aunt Meg I've already grabbed something on the fly?"

"Jeff doesn't want to see me," she reminded Mrs. Roberts when her father had left the office.

"Just please get here."

"What's so wrong all of a sudden?"

"More of the same except…he's deeply depressed and he's been drinking. And the hands in the stables aren't doing their jobs. I just had a horse on the breakfast room terrace."

Hope had to pause a moment to get a handle on that piece of information. "A horse on the terrace? And what do you mean he's drinking? Jeff's parents were killed by a drunk driver. He doesn't drink. Ever. Not even to be sociable."

"Tell him that. This has been going on for about a week. He gets that guard he hired to bring it to him. But today Reginald Boyer is here. Jeff got one of the men to bring him downstairs. I think Boyer's angling to buy Mr. March. He was in a nasty mood with me then all sweetness and light with Jeff. I'm afraid of what's going to happen if Boyer convinces Jeff. He needs the dream, at least. And I'm afraid of what Mr. Boyer will say if Jeff continues to refuse.''

Hope's heart froze as she recalled Jeff telling the nurse to give him an overdose. Jeff was alone and vulnerable. No matter how angry he was at her, Hope knew she couldn't let that man take away Jeff's last vestige of hope. ''Make sure the gates are open,'' she told Mrs. Roberts as she stood.

She made a grab for her jacket as she hung up the phone, then barreled out of her office and right into her father's chest.

''Hope, you can't go over there,'' he said, a mutinous expression on his face.

''Listening at doors now, Dad?'' she asked, trying to tamp down her annoyance.

''I'm only trying to protect you from making a huge mistake.''

''Who asked you to? And Jeff is not a mistake!''

He sighed. ''Hope, he's not worth it. He'll only cause you heartache. All he cares about is having fun and spending money.''

Hope stared at her father. Where did he get these ideas? ''You have no idea what Jeff's really like because you've never given him a chance. I doubt you've had a civil word to say about him or to him since Cole was arrested.''

''This has nothing to do with Cole. It has to do with you being in love with a bored playboy who'll do nothing but cause you grief and waste your life!''

"Jeff isn't spoiled or lazy."

"No? Then why does he just sit over there on that estate? Why has he refused to even try getting better? Because he's always just drifted along and done the easiest thing."

"You don't know him! Now get out of my way. He needs me."

Ross grabbed her arm when she tried to sidestep him. "I'm not letting you go over there to waste your time on him."

Hope shook him off. "It's my time to waste. I am not a child and I'm not letting you pick my friends for me. It's none of your business."

"It *is* my business if you go over there during working hours. I don't pay you to play nursemaid to a spoiled cripple."

That did it! She started forward, throwing her reply over her shoulder. "I'll be back before lunch hour's over, and if not, you can dock my pay!"

Chapter Four

Pale and visibly upset, Mrs. Roberts opened the front door of Jeff's imposing neoclassical home. Hope's temper, which had already been flowing at full throttle, shot to an all-time high. She'd struggled long and hard with her temper and with the Lord's help had mostly mastered it, but seeing how upset Emily Roberts was undid a lot of work.

Mrs. Roberts dragged Hope across the marble foyer with a forceful grip, leading her toward the front parlor. "That Mr. Boyer's getting nasty, just as I feared. He hid his mood with Jeff till just a few minutes ago, but he was vicious about our boy. He said he'd been careless or he'd never have been hurt."

Hope felt a fierce stab of guilt pierce her heart. It hadn't been Jeff's carelessness but her own.

"He was vile about it when he first arrived. Luckily, Jeff was still upstairs. Please don't let him say anything too upsetting to Jeffrey's face. It'll break what's left of his spirit. I just know it.''

Hope took a few calming breaths. It wouldn't do to charge in like a half-crazed mare. ''Take it easy, Mrs. R,'' she said. ''I'll see if I can divert things a bit. If Jeff doesn't toss me out first, that is.''

Hope rushed ahead, determined to be as civil and pleasant as possible, but she felt her blood pressure rise when she heard Boyer's cutting voice emanate from the room ahead. She reached one of the columns that stood sentinel in the doorway of the front parlor. She gripped the cool marble, her fingertips turning white as she tried to tone down her temper.

''Honestly, Jeffrey. You're being childish,'' Reginald Boyer said. ''Mr. March does not belong rusticating in the country or serving as a stud. He lives for competition. Gary Johnson has a shot at moving up in the standings with a better animal. You're useless to the team now, but you could make this one last contribution. Don't be so selfish. You're no good to the animal anymore. Really, when was the last time you exercised him?''

''I can't walk, Reggie,'' Jeff replied, his tone flat. ''Obviously I'm not the one caring for him. Or exercising him.''

''He's worthless to anyone out here eating grass and wasting away. As worthless as—''

''Don't you dare finish that, Mr. Boyer.'' Hope burst in, unable to contain her anger a second longer. She stood at the entrance to the room, anger pulsing through her. After letting go of the column beneath her fingers, she moved forward and down the two steps into the sitting area.

"What kind of man are you to come here and purposely demoralize Jeff just to get your way? Talk about selfish. Mr. March is not for sale. Take your poison personality and get out. Jeff doesn't need you coming around to make him feel worse."

"On what authority are you telling me to leave?" Reginald Boyer asked, his back stiff, his tone pompous and superior.

Hope glanced at Jeff for the first time. His handsome face looked haggard, and his beautifully sculpted jaw and chin were covered by a scraggly beard that had to represent weeks of growth. He stared straight ahead, his eyes clearly seeing nothing but his own thoughts—and those were obviously dark ones. Hope wasn't sure he even knew she was there. He was a remnant of his former self. And it was all her fault.

She looked away, the sight too painful to deal with just then. Instead she turned her attention to Jeff's former coach. "On the authority of someone who cares about Jeff. On the authority of someone who loves him and won't allow you to destroy what's left of him. He certainly isn't protesting my interference, is he?"

Boyer shook his shoulders as if straightening his jacket but said nothing, so Hope continued. "Jeff doesn't deserve to have you come here and try to take away the last of his pride and hope. He'll ride Mr. March again and he can't do that if the horse is gone. Go find your new rising star his own mount. He can't have Jeff's.''

Boyer gave her a cold-eyed stare and tried to walk closer to where Jeff sat. But Hope had given ground for the last time where Jeff's best interests were concerned. She should never have stayed away. She boldly stepped to the side and blocked Boyer's way.

She stared into his cold black eyes. ''I asked you to leave,'' she said, her voice as cold as her temper was hot. ''Get out before I call Cole to come throw you out.''

''I do not like to be threatened, Ms. Taggert.''

Hope smiled coolly. ''I'm appalled that you think I'd threaten you. I was actually making you a promise. Mrs. Roberts, will you see the gentleman out? Good day, Mr. Boyer.''

Boyer stared at her for several long moments, and Hope stared right back. Only when he'd turned away and stomped out did Hope approach Jeff. She prayed for the wisdom and words to reach him.

''Jeff, why would you let him talk to you that way?'' she demanded, sitting in a chair near him.

He blinked then looked at her, but his eyes took on no more life than when he'd been staring at nothing. ''Ever hear the expression about not shooting the messenger?'' he asked, his tone as flat as when he'd spoken to Boyer. ''I couldn't very well refute what he said. Or what he was about to say. I *am* worthless, after all.''

''That isn't true!''

"To Mr. March I am. I want you to take him to Laurel Glen. Bring over a boarding agreement."

"Jeff, why? You have exercise boys and stable hands, too."

"Because I don't want to see him out there standing around bored or pacing like a nervous chicken. It'll ruin him."

"You're giving up. You worked so hard to get on the Olympic team. And to develop a name in breeding. Why can't you work as hard to get back on your feet again?"

"Been there. Done that," he said flippantly. "Do me a favor before you go, get me a beer."

Hope stood and fisted her hands on her hips. "No. I will not get you a beer. What on earth are you doing to yourself? You don't drink. I've always respected that you took that stand about alcohol after your parents were killed by that drunk driver."

"Come on, Hope. I'm not exactly driving these days, am I? Unless...do you want to count the chair?" His grin was insolent as he pushed the control switch on the chair forward and came at her—full throttle. Hope was momentarily stunned and pivoted just in time to avoid him running in to her. Jeff quickly spun the chair and laughed as he came after her again. It wasn't a happy sound.

"I'm not playing your game, Jeff Carrington!" she shouted and stomped up the steps. "Come and get me here," she challenged.

Furious Jeff gave chase and let the chair smack into the bottom step of living room just below Hope's booted feet. The room spun when he looked at her— a blurred figure in denim and suede. He was thankful he couldn't see her face clearly. There was only so much a man could take. He didn't want to see disillusionment on her face even though he was trying to chase her away.

"Why are you here?" he asked and hated the slight slur in his voice. "I told you I don't want you smothering me. Poor Jeff. Let's cheer up poor Jeff. Let's smile for poor Jeff. Let's lie to poor Jeff if we have to, but we have to keep his spirits up. Here's a news flash for you, Hope. I don't want your sympathy, your patience or your fake smile. I don't need smothering! I want to be left alone."

For just a moment her face came into focus and she smiled a real true smile. For just a moment he felt a shred of happiness.

"You're right," she said. "You don't need smothering, and I'm sorry if that's all you felt from me. I'm going to give you what you say you need. I'll be back with that agreement."

He frowned and watched her go. "That was too easy," he told Mrs. Roberts. "Much too easy."

"You should be careful or you might find out that you've managed to send away all the best people in your life."

He stared at the older woman with the round figure and graying hair. He didn't think she'd changed a bit in all the years she'd been with him. "Get me a beer, will you?"

Mrs. Roberts frowned. "Please don't make me feed my boy that mind poison."

"I'll get Billy to handle it for me." Jeff laughed. "Mind poison? Where do you get this stuff? No wonder I keep you around. You're a regular laugh riot, Mrs. R."

"You keep me around because no one else loves you the way I do. You remember that when you're calling yourself worthless and useless. You're my sweetheart. Have been ever since the day you toddled into my kitchen looking for cookies. You remember that!" she ordered.

Jeff grimaced. Everyone who opened their mouth near him today reminded him. "I can't toddle anymore, Mrs. R."

"It wasn't the toddling that won my heart. It was that smile. I'm off to get a start on dinner. Be good."

She smiled that gentle smile of hers and went off to do what he paid her to do. Jeff found himself fighting tears. He'd always wished she was family and not paid to be with him. Growing up, his greatest fear was that she would leave him. She was all he had left.

Hope knew she had to do something. What Jeff said was true. She hadn't responded to any of his barbs as she normally would, and she'd done it right from the first. She and Cole had left when Jeff had asked rather than risk upsetting him the evening of the accident. She should have stood her ground and dared him to do his worst. She knew what she'd done wrong but hadn't a clue how to fix it.

She pulled the Jeep next to the barn where she kept her office. She longed for the warmth of the rich old knotty pine paneling and the smell of the wood fire simmering in the cast-iron stove in the corner. She wanted to hide. To curl up on the worn hunter-green leather sofa with a warm woolen blanket and just let the atmosphere chase away the chill of Jeff's marble edifice.

Entering, she found her brother on the phone behind her desk. He looked up and quickly got off the phone.

"So how was it?" he asked. "Dad was bouncing off the walls because you went over there. I gather you had quite a confrontation."

Hope tried to choke back the tears that had been threatening since she saw Jeff's dissipated condition. "He looks awful. Why didn't you tell me?" she asked, and then she lost it. She felt her face crumple along with her composure. Cole was at her side in seconds, and she was soaking his shirt just as quickly.

"Oh, sweetheart, I didn't want to hurt you," he murmured, then tightened his hold on her and let her cry.

"I knew no good would come of her going over there," Ross growled from the doorway. "I told her he'd only hurt her."

Nothing had ever stopped Hope's tears faster than anger. She pushed out of Cole's embrace and rounded on her father. "He didn't do anything to hurt me. It's the way he is that hurts. That and knowing I did it to him. You're so wrapped up in your little prejudices that you can't see the truth. This was all my fault. I feel responsible. I *am* responsible. And I have to help him.''

"Hope, you can't make Jeff care," Cole said. "I've talked till I'm blue in the face, but he won't listen."

"Have you tried to *make* him listen?"

Cole held out his hands helplessly. "What do you want me to do? Scream at a man in a wheelchair?"

She could hear Jeff's words. *I don't need smothering.* "Maybe," she said thoughtfully. "Maybe that's what he needs."

"What he needs," Ross said, as if Hope hadn't spoken, "is a good swift kick."

"Exactly, Daddy," Hope said with a sudden smile. "And I'm going to figure out how to give it to him."

"I've had it. I want you to stay away from him!" Ross ordered.

"I told you earlier." She paused and glared at her father. "What I do with my life is my business. I refuse to let you tell me who I can and who I can't care for. This is *my* decision. My life. And I'm going to do what I have to do to wake Jeff up to the possibilities that are still open to him."

"You're a fool!" Ross shouted, stalking away.

The room fell silent, and Hope stared through the glass between her office and the rest of the barn, wondering what she could do.

"That went well," Cole quipped as he leaned against the desk, his hands negligently stuffed in the front pockets of his khakis. He shook his head. "I can't believe I thought you let him run your life. I was so jealous of your relationship with him. And now I find out that you two really go at it."

Hope arched one eyebrow. "Yes, but unlike you, I've learned to pick my battles. And this is one of those issues I can't back down on."

"So what are you up to?" Cole asked. "I remember that look."

Hope shook her head. "I don't know yet. Jeff wants to board Mr. March here, so I have to go over to Lavender Hill with an agreement."

"Why is March coming here?"

Walking to the filing cabinet, Hope thought of all she'd learned today. "Because Jeff doesn't want to look at him. Besides, since Jeff's fired anyone who'd care if he got better, no animal is really safe there. I imagine you've seen the crew he's hired as replacements. Mrs. Roberts probably has to count the silver after any of them are in the house, and today one of the mares wandered as far as the back terrace."

As Hope looked for the standard boarding agreement, she noticed a power of attorney that she often had clients sign if they were leaving on a trip. If anything happened to a horse, Laurel Glen needed to be able to act as agent of the owners to get treatment.

"I wish I had power of attorney for Jeff's care. I'd toss half that crew of his out the door and get things back to normal over there," she grumbled, hooking a thick lock of hair behind her ear. She stared at the agreements. They looked nearly identical.

Could it be this easy?

"A word changed here," she murmured, "a word there."

"Hope, you've really got that look now," Cole said from his slouched seat on the old sofa. "And every time you've ever had it, you've done something outlandish."

"He needs someone riding him twenty-four seven. And it has to be someone who wants what's best for him. Someone strong enough to do what needs to be done and not bow to his will. Someone who wants him to get better as much, if not more, than he does right now. And someone who can run a farm."

She turned and reached for the phone. "Mrs. R, it's Hope. Is the homestead house unoccupied?"

Hope glanced in her rearview mirror at Laurel Glen. She still couldn't believe her father had fired her. Hope knew he'd regret it and the harsh things he'd said. She was sorry she'd driven him to act so rashly, but she had to do this.

She loved Jeff and she had to get him to help himself. Even if she had no feelings beyond friendship, she'd still have to help. It was her fault he was in the condition he was in and therefore her fault his animals were endangered. She had to make things better.

Her plan was a bold one and sure to get as strong a reaction from Jeff as it had from her father. She had warned her father not to ask her to choose between the man she loved and him. And she would just as readily explain to him another truth she'd learned lately. Peace at any price is not worth it. Jeff might hate her by the time she left, but as sure as her name was Hope Taggert, he would at least care about life again!

Chapter Five

Hope stood for a second outside Jeff's room. She looked at the piece of paper in her hand and closed her eyes. *Please forgive this deception, Lord. I won't lie but I can't tell him the truth, either. This is for his own good. I have to get him to take a good hard look at what he's doing to himself.*

Hope took a deep breath and knocked. When no answer came, she knocked again—harder this time.

"What?" Jeff's voice snapped from within.

"It's Hope. I have the agreement," she called, then entered when he told her to come in. She nearly gasped when she saw the room—smelled the room. It was worse than a locker room. She'd smelled stables that were fresher and was sure there were trash dumps that were more orderly. As she approached the bed, Hope realized that it wasn't only the room in need of a good scrubbing.

She looked at Jeff. He lay on the bed, still wearing

the T-shirt he'd had on earlier in the day. From the looks of things, it was the same one he'd had on all week. He was haphazardly covered to the waist by a wrinkled sheet. His hair was matted and needed a good washing, and the scraggly beard still hid much of his handsome face.

Mrs. R had warned her that the room was as much a mess as Jeff, but she hadn't believed it. Now she did. She'd wondered where to start. Well, she had her answer.

But there were preparations for the campaign to get him to straighten up and fly right that she and Cole had mapped out. And getting the agreement signed was the first step. Holding her breath, Hope handed Jeff the contract and a pen.

He blinked his eyes, leafed through the pages and sighed. "How much a year?" he asked, annoyed.

She named the standard boarding fee at Laurel Glen. She hadn't lied. Not yet. But Mr. March wouldn't be making a move. Because Hope already had. Into Lavender Hill's quaint little homestead house.

Jeff scribbled his name on the last page and handed it to her. "That's it then?" he asked.

Hope nodded. She'd file the papers in the morning. But today she intended to clean house. Not literally, she thought, looking around at the room's early American trash dump decor. Literal cleaning would come soon enough.

"I'll be seeing you," she told him after examining his signature.

"What, no comment?" Jeff demanded and took a swig from a beer someone obviously had brought him. She doubted it had been Mrs. Roberts. Enjoy it, Hope thought, looking at the amber-colored bottle in his hand. It'll be your last.

Hope put her hand on her hip. "You expect a comment? About this?" She gestured to the room. "It just confirms what I've heard. You've decided to not only wallow in self-pity but to do it in a pigsty while you're at it. I'll see you tomorrow."

Tempted to make an unwise comment about what he could expect tomorrow to be like, Hope turned on her heels and left. Out in the hall, she leaned against the wall. Billy, the guard who had been toting and fetching for Jeff as well as screening his visitors, was the first on her list of things to go.

Jeff closed his eyes and let his head drop back against the headboard. Does the torture never end? Just when he'd thought he'd figured out how to get from one day to the next, he had to go and have a day like this. First Reggie stopped by and brought home just how worthless he was and made him remember all the yesterdays that were gone. Then, when he was about to really lose it, Hope had to go and ride to the rescue. Not only had it been humiliating, but seeing her again had reminded him of all the tomorrows he'd lost, too.

He glanced at the bottle in his hand, then tipped it to his lips, draining it. If only this stuff didn't taste so lousy, his new life master plan wouldn't be so bad.

He reached next to the bed and pulled another amber-colored bottle out of the little refrigerator he'd had Billy fill that morning. By dark, or a little after, he ought to be able to sleep. The alcohol numbed not only his mind to the past and future but the knotted muscles in his legs and back. And when the numbness came, one more day would be over.

Just like his life.

"Well, look who's up bright and early this morning," Mrs. R said with a pleasant smile the next morning as Hope walked through the back door into the Italian country kitchen. The kitchen and breakfast room were a homey enclave from the cold starkness of the rest of the house.

"What do you plan to do today?" Mrs. R continued as she poured a cup of coffee and walked with it to the table. "Are you going to replace the staff you gave the axe yesterday?"

Hope shook her head. "I already called the agency my aunt Meg uses. I gave them the names and numbers of everyone you thought we should hire back if we can. They're going to handle the rest of that. Unfortunately when I called Gus Peoples, he said he was already working and feels he can't break his contract, so I guess I'm running the stables now. They sent temps for us till we get everything back to normal. At least today you won't have Sally's Fortune stomping around the back door.

"The next thing on my agenda is to get rid of that gorilla at the front gate. I'm looking forward to it. I took a look at the petty cash ledger last night. His math is inventive, I'll give him that much. After that happy task is over, I'll tackle the really tough job.''

Mrs. R's eyebrows rose, wrinkling her brow. ''Oh. What would that be?''

Hope took a deep breath. ''Mrs. R, I—''

Mrs. R put her hand on Hope's shoulder. ''Dear, if you're going to be living here helping my Jeffrey find himself again, don't you think we could dispense with the Mrs. R? It's Emily. Please.''

Hope nodded. ''Emily it is, then. I do want to help Jeff. But Jeff has to want to help himself, too. First thing this morning, I called Curtis Madden from church. I was hoping he'd be free and, praise the Lord, he is. He's looking for a long-term assignment. I gave him one. Jeff. Curt's a good nurse and an even better physical therapist. This is the type of work he trained for. He'll be here at nine and ready for a challenge.''

''Challenge? You aren't going to upset Jeff, are you?'' Emily asked and sank to a chair at the table. Hope saw that her hands shook. She sat across from Emily and took one of her increasingly frail hands in her own. This had to be so painful for her. She loved Jeff like a son, yet she had no say in how he went about his life.

Hope checked her watch. She had promised Emily that she'd get Jeff moving ahead in life again. But she hadn't outlined her tough-love idea yet. Without Emily's help and cooperation, this plan would fail. While Hope hated to see the older woman upset, she hated to see Jeff waste the gift of his life more. A lot more.

"Yesterday," she began, "I got Jeff's signature on a power of attorney, but he thinks he signed a Laurel Glen boarding agreement for Mr. March."

Emily's wrinkled brow scrunched with her worried frown. "I don't understand, dear."

"Jeff needs help whether he wants it or not. And he doesn't want it. You know it. I know it. He's given up. It's our job to make him want to get better. Being nice and giving him room and time to come to grips with the accident isn't working. He's gaining weight and losing muscle mass every day. There's no time to tiptoe around this. The most important month of his recovery is already wasted. That's why we're changing the staff back to people who care about him. He doesn't know what I've done. When everything is in place, he will. Are you ready for the explosion?"

"He'll be furious. Oh, Hope, I don't know about this."

"Mrs. R, Emily, do you trust me? Do you believe I love Jeff too much to take advantage of the power of attorney?"

The housekeeper looked surprised. "Of course, I do. That isn't an issue."

"Good, because the president of First Nation will be here any minute."

"The president of Jeff's bank?"

Hope nodded as the back door opened.

"Hey, what are you doing here?" Billy Dever, the

soon-to-be unemployed security guard, asked. "You aren't on the *A* list."

Hope stood and smiled. "There have been a few changes in the *A* list since you left yesterday, Mr. Dever. Would you come to the study with me? We need to have a chat. Emily, if the gentleman I mentioned arrives, please show him to the front parlor and tell him I'll be with him any minute."

Moments later Hope took a seat behind the ebony desk in Jeff's study and motioned Billy Dever to the chair facing her. "I won't beat around the bush with you, Mr. Dever. Your services are no longer required at Lavender Hill. Here is a check for two months' wages. I'm sorry for the abruptness of this dismissal, but I'm sure someone as conscientious as you will be able to find employment in that amount of time."

"I'm fired? You can't do that! Carrington hired me."

"I beg to differ." Hope handed him a copy of the power of attorney Jeff had mistakenly signed the evening before. "As you can see, Mr. Carrington has placed his welfare and Lavender Hill's in my hands. And having you here, sir, is *not* in his best interests. As for unemployment compensation, I think your creative accounting speaks for itself. I wouldn't try to file a claim. If you do I may be forced to speak to the district attorney about the discrepancies I found in the petty cash account." Hope stood. "Have a nice day."

Dever glanced at the agreement in stunned silence,

then at her with narrowed eyes. "I knew you were trouble."

"It's my middle name, Mr. Dever." Hope stood, fighting a smile. It was a clear dismissal. Even someone of Billy Dever's ilk knew that.

Having heard the door chimes ring just after she gave Dever his walking papers, Hope headed for the front parlor. After a short visit to Jeff's room, the banker was only too happy to help his old friends' grandson any way he could. Tough love, he'd said, was clearly better than the status quo.

"What's next?" Emily asked.

"Jeff." Hope took a deep breath. "Curt should be here any minute. Send him up, will you? Oh, and where do you keep the trash bags?"

"Rise and shine, lazybones!"

Jeff found himself blasted out of sleep. A voice— Hope's voice—reverberated in his head like a gong. Then light flooded the room and thrust a thousand knives into his skull.

"What the—" The curse word froze on his lips when he opened his eyes and saw Hope, her hair bouncing with every movement, throw open the terrace doors. Then she moved to the windows across from his bed and opened them, too. The icy fingers of March followed. He closed his eyes. His head was pounding. "Go away and let a man die in peace. What are you doing? Are you trying to torture me?"

"What I am doing is shaping you up, Carrington.

And first things first." She walked to the terrace. "You all set down there, Manny?"

"All set, Ms. Taggert," Lavender Hill's gardener, jack-of-all-trades and helper of all—whether they wanted help or not—shouted.

Jeff frowned, keeping his eyes closed against the sunlight, and tried to order his thoughts. There was more wrong with this scene than Hope being in his room, opening windows and trying to blast the head off his shoulders. Oh, if only beer didn't leave him so fuzzy and achy headed after a couple six-packs. What was he saying? Fuzzy-headed mornings—a fuzzy-headed life—were what he was looking for.

"Manny. I fired Manny," he said, figuring out one inconsistency. Manny had been the first one he'd let go. His cheer and enthusiasm had been too much to bear.

"And I rehired him." Hope chirped the words gleefully, then turned back to Manny. "I'll toss the trash left and the clothes right. Just stuff it all in the plastic bags. Mrs. Roberts will see to the clothes, and you can handle the trash."

"I gave him six months' severance. And hey, why are you tossing my stuff out the window? I like my room just the way it is."

"Honestly, Jeff, I've smelled stables more pleasant than this room," Hope complained. "I didn't intend to subject anyone else to this. It can be sorted in the fresh air just as easily."

"No one invited you in here. Get out. And hey! What do you mean, you rehired him? You don't have the right to hire and fire people around here. You're fired, Manny,'' Jeff shouted.

''*Si*, Mr. Carrington. Whatever you say, Mr. Carrington,'' Manny called, sounding entirely too happy to have just lost his income.

Jeff watched in impotent fury as Hope gathered more of his clothes.

''Actually,'' she said as she heaved the pile over the balcony into the fresh air she seemed to crave, ''I do have the right to hire and fire around here. You gave it to me yesterday when you signed the power of attorney I brought over.''

''What power of attorney? The only thing I signed was a boarding agreement.''

''You really shouldn't drink. Not only is it an unappealing trait but it impairs your faculties.'' Hope grinned and walked toward the side of the bed where Billy had replaced the nightstand with a neat little dorm fridge. She eyed it suspiciously.

Jeff glanced at the fridge that still contained a six-pack. ''Where's Billy? Billy!'' he bellowed.

''Billy is probably off celebrating his good fortune. You see, rather than being arrested for petty theft, he got two months' severance pay.''

''You fired him? I need him. He helps me. You think I can get dressed on my own? Get into the bathroom on my own?''

Hope gave him a sour look. ''It's clear that even with Mr. Dever's help you've been unable to get as far as the tub. Today all that will change.''

Jeff spat out a foul oath and reached for the phone.

Hope was faster. He watched in horror as she yanked on the cord and pulled it out of the wall then tossed the phone over the terrace railing.

"Heads up, Manny!" she shouted as his only means of rescue sailed off for points unknown.

"This is kidnapping," Jeff charged.

Hope raised that infernal eyebrow that always made her look so imperious and stared at him. "So far I haven't had you moved even an inch."

"I'll have you tossed in prison. Your father would just love it if you followed in big brother's footsteps. I'll tell the police I'm being held against my will and that you misrepresented that agreement. That's fraud!"

She folded her arms. "Prove it," she challenged. "Emily signed as a witness. Are you going to toss her in jail, too? Just for caring about your welfare?"

Okay, indignant didn't work. Maybe pitiful would. "Hope, you can't do this. How can you take advantage of me like this?" he asked, pitifully. He could have sworn twin flames replaced Hope's blue eyes. He stared at her, his eyes still not quite focusing correctly.

"I can do this because I care about you, Jeff. I'm *not* letting you go on this way."

Jeff watched in helpless dread as she bent, opened the fridge and scowled. As if having her yank the phone out wasn't bad enough. "No!"

Hope bent over him till they were nose to nose. His sweet Hope had turned into the drill instructor from his worst nightmares. "Oh, yes. You want to stop me? Get out of that bed and make me."

"You know I can't do that!" To his humiliation, his voice broke. To cover the emotions Jeff fought on a daily basis, he flopped back in the bed and looked away.

"What I know is that you're not *trying* to get out of that bed. You're wallowing. In grimy sheets. In trash and dirty clothes. In filth! And worst of all, in self-pity. And it ends. Here! Now!"

Oh, he was really mad. Who did she think she was standing there—*standing* there—telling him he was wallowing in self-pity? So what if he was? He had a right. If she couldn't see that, it was her problem.

"And how do you think you're going to get me to do what you want? Are you going to haul my carcass out of this bed? Are you going to change the sheets? Give me a bath?" he taunted, expecting her to blush and run from the room.

But he was wrong. Again. A tap on the door drew their attention, but not before Hope glared at him instead of cowering, her expression annoyingly determined. Her complexion hadn't darkened even a shade, either.

"Come in, Curt. Join the party. This is your patient, Jeffrey Carrington. Jeff, this is Curtis Madden. He prefers to be called Curt."

Jeff watched in horror as a large man with muscles on his muscles, wearing navy surgical scrubs, strode into the room. On his pleasant face was a warm smile. Jeff scowled at the man.

"Do me a favor, will you, Curt?" Hope said. "Haul that nice little fridge out to my cottage. I could use something to keep soft drinks by my bed. It'll make those middle-of-the-night refrigerator raids much easier."

Jeff watched in amazement as the big hulking blond strode in and removed his lifeline to oblivion. He wouldn't miss the lousy taste, just its mind- and body-numbing effects. Just as Madden stepped into the hall, what she'd said cut through the rest of the fog in his brain. Her cottage? He narrowed his eyes.

"What cottage?"

"The cottage out back. Lavender Hill's homestead house. It was your grandparents' home, if memory serves."

"You aren't moving in there."

"Too late. Already have," she quipped.

"Then move out. Ross'll be furious. He's liable to fire you."

"Too late. Already is. Already has."

He groaned. If Ross hadn't been able to stop her, nothing he said would dissuade her from this campaign of hers. But he could still do plenty. Like resist. Like make her life miserable. The only problem was he'd cut off his association with her to keep himself from making her miserable. Well, what was the old saying? Sometimes you have to be cruel to be kind.

"You're pathetic. How desperate are you for a man if you'll go this far to get one—even one who's worthless? Didn't your aunt Meg teach you that it's gauche to throw yourself at someone?"

Jeff congratulated himself when anger flared in her blue eyes. But his triumph withered and died as soon as she gave words to her fury—disappointing words.

"I won't listen to you calling yourself worthless. You say that one more time and I swear I'll put pepper on your tongue."

"You and what army?" he replied, then looked up as the hulk—Kirk, was it?—strode into the room. "You going to get the captain here to hold me down?"

"He's here to help you. I don't need help. Now I imagine it's bath time. I'll see you boys later."

Jeff growled as she left then turned his gaze on Madden. "So, how much am I paying you to humiliate me?"

The young man in the surgical scrubs stood at the foot of the bed and crossed his meaty arms. "I'm not here to humiliate you, Mr. Carrington."

"Come on, Captain Kirk, you're apparently going to see me in my altogether. Make it Jeff. Why stand on ceremony?"

Madden nodded. "All right. Jeff it is then. And I'm Curt, or Curtis, or nurse. Not Captain Kirk—unless *you're* trying to embarrass *me*. You asked why I'm here. I'm here to either help you get better or to help you learn to cope with your disability. I'm an RN and I have a degree in physical therapy. And I specialize in cases like yours."

Jeff frowned. What kind of life was that for a twenty-something, good-looking guy? "Helping cripples learn to go on in the world? Is that your thing?"

Jeff asked, pulling sarcasm around him like a shield. Madden's blue eyes seemed to see too much, though, and it made Jeff decidedly uncomfortable.

"No. I specialize in tough cases, Jeff."

"Ah. Now I see. Cases that don't have a snowball's chance at the equator of getting better. Like me."

Madden leaned down and braced his hands on the footboard of Jeff's sleigh bed. "No, Jeff. Cases where the patient won't try and can't seem to care enough to see what their self-pity is doing to those around them. You ready for your bath?" he asked. "I'm told you don't get fed till you're clean and smelling fresh as a daisy." He sniffed the air. "I'd say we have a lot of work in that area."

Hope waited till Curt let her know he had Jeff in the tub before she stripped the bed. She had finished clearing the debris from the bureau and chest and making the bed with clean linens when the therapist came in looking for a clean towel and clothes. Luckily there were plenty of both.

Half an hour later, Jeff had still not appeared in the breakfast room. Mrs. Roberts, excited that he'd be eating downstairs, had gone all out with his favorites—an omelette, fruit salad and fresh coffee cake. Not knowing whether to be worried or annoyed, Hope returned to his clean inner sanctum, and all thoughts of worry fled when she overheard him talking to Curt.

"I eat in my room. I told you. I'm not well enough to be dragged up and down the stairs all the time. Just go get me a tray. I'm hungry. And I haven't had my coffee.''

Hope turned on her heels and went to the kitchen. How could he care so little about Emily? Jeff had never treated her like anything other than a grandmother, and suddenly he'd begun treating her like his parents had. Like the help.

Well, fine. If he wanted to be treated like an invalid, she'd feed him like an invalid. Maybe that would wake him up!

She stalked into the kitchen and pulled out a pot. Next she hunted up the oatmeal she knew had to be there. Not because Emily would ever serve it for breakfast but because she made the best oatmeal cookies in two counties. And they weren't nearly as good as her omelettes. Jeff didn't know what he was missing.

But he soon would.

''What on earth are you up to now?'' Emily Roberts asked, worry evident in her voice.

''He says he's not well enough to come down. With a little change in the menu I'm going to demonstrate the difference between being well and being so sick you're confined to bed.''

Luckily, Emily stocked quick-cooking oatmeal, so Jeff's breakfast was ready in less than five minutes. Hope loaded a tray and carried it upstairs and into his room.

''You're not up to coming down yet, I hear,'' she said, her voice full of sympathy. ''So I brought up some breakfast fit for an invalid. I think you'll enjoy it. I brought mine along so we could visit."

Hope made a great production of settling the tray across his lap then she lifted the plate with her omelette and handed Jeff his spoon.

He frowned, dipped into the oatmeal and lifted the spoon, tilting it to the side and letting the contents plop into the bowl. "What's this? And what am I supposed to do with it? Hire a paperhanger?"

Hope chuckled. At least some of his sense of humor was still intact. "It's oatmeal. Not wallpaper paste. Aunt Meg always says hot cereal really sticks to your ribs. And I added some nice stewed prunes. And tea with a drop of milk. Just what your delicate constitution needs."

Jeff's frown turned to a full-fledged scowl. "But you have one of Mrs. R's omelettes."

"Yes, I do. But then I'm not the one too weak to go to the breakfast room."

His eyes lit with fury. "Torture! You're trying to torture me. That's it! Admit it!"

A sadness so profound fell like a shadow over Hope, and she nearly burst into tears. No one ever warned her that tough love hurt the one on the administering side more than the receiver. Jeff was genuinely angry and, from his point of view, rightly so. She was the usurper, never mind that she was only trying to help, and to his mind he was doing just fine.

Hope took a deep breath and stood. "I'm trying to show you that there are things you can do to lead a productive, useful life and that you aren't doing them.''

''Whose idea of a productive life? Yours? What do you know about what I'm capable of doing? I'm not *able* to do a thing on my own! Nothing. And you know nothing whatever about me or my capabilities.''

She shook her head and walked to the bed, carrying the untouched omelette. She put it on the tray and picked up the cereal bowl. ''Here's your breakfast, Jeff. I was just trying to make a point about how *well* you really are. And there's another point to eating downstairs. Do you think it's easy for Mrs. Roberts to schlep your trays up and down that flight and a half of stairs three times a day? Why don't you take the rest of the day to sulk up here? Curt can work on beginning your therapy today.''

Hope took a deep breath and stiffened her resolve. Hard or easy, she couldn't back down yet. He was worth every second of her own pain and discomfort. ''But it's a one-day reprieve,'' she continued. ''To-morrow you find a way to get downstairs or I'll know the reason why not!''

Chapter Six

On her way to convince Jeff to eat the evening meal downstairs, Hope heard Curt's voice float into the hall outside the room.

"Come on, Jeff," he urged. "Try one more time."

Jeff expelled a quick breath seconds later, and she heard the crisp sheets rustle. "I can't do it. My arms feel like jelly. I can't even get myself into a wheelchair." Jeff laughed, but it was once again sadly a bitter sound. "How worthless is that? I even fail at being a cripple."

Hope closed her eyes and blocked out Curt offering to lift him into the chair and Jeff's sharp negative retort. *Lord,* she prayed, *it hurts to hear him sound so down and discouraged, but he has to keep trying. Giving up on life isn't an option. What do I do to show him the way?*

What she really wanted to do was to go in there and hug him. To offer comfort. But that was what *she* wanted. One by one scenes from earlier in the day replayed themselves and she stiffened her resolved. Comfort wasn't what he needed. She'd done what she'd done so far to help him. And help him she would.

Turning on her heel, Hope followed the wonderful scent of Emily's cooking to the kitchen. She'd warned him, she told herself. He wouldn't be able to say she hadn't.

"Yum. That smells wonderful," Hope said as she lifted a pot lid and sniffed the gumbo Emily had been preparing for hours. "I don't think Jeff's going to be down for dinner tonight, either. But don't worry. I'll take it up to him."

"That's nice, dear," Emily said as she bent, pot holder in hand, to peer into the oven. "I'll have the baguettes out of the oven in two shakes of a lamb's tail. If you put a little butter on a bread plate, they'll be ready to go."

Hope took care of the butter and the bread plate then dished up a serving of Emily's famous gumbo. With the full dish, she walked calmly to the spice cabinet. She wouldn't need to have Curt hold Jeff down at all. He was about to dole out his own consequences all by himself. She felt her lips twitch.

"What are you doing?" Emily asked.

"Keeping a promise," Hope explained and shook out a few healthy splashes of jalapeño hot sauce onto the top of Jeff's dinner. She stirred it in only enough to disguise its presence, then picked up the tray as Emily settled the plate holding the fresh baguette and a pat of butter. "I'd have a big glass of milk ready. But don't bring it up right away. His object lesson shouldn't end too soon."

Hope sighed. The older woman's frown and worried eyes gave her pause. Maybe she shouldn't. She looked at the laced gumbo. "He said it again. Called himself worthless. It hurts hearing him so down on himself, especially when I caused the accident. I just want him to stop and think before he says something so untrue about himself. Maybe if he isn't saying it, he'll stop believing it."

"Jeffrey doesn't blame you in the least. As for the hot sauce, maybe he does need shaking up. He can't keep repeating and believing his father's criticisms or he'll waste away in that bed. Hearing him call himself worthless is like an old nightmare come back to haunt me. I thought he'd gotten far beyond all those childhood hurts, but I guess children never lose the scars of their early years."

Hope silently denounced Addison Carrington for his cruelty. The man hadn't been a father to Jeff, but a scourge, and his negligent mother hadn't been much better. Glancing at the doctored gumbo, Hope grew more comfortable with the course of action.

She wasn't being cruel. She was trying to make him see how very much he *was* worth. They called it tough love. Just as military school had broken Cole out of his destructive behavior, she hoped and prayed her version would do the same for Jeff's brand of the same malignant pattern her brother had once engaged in. Her resolve strengthened, Hope carried the bed tray upstairs and pasted a smile on her face.

"Dinner," she called as she entered the room. Jeff was still in the bed, and Curt sat next to him in a chair. Both men looked up.

"See? Even Hope doesn't expect me to make it downstairs for dinner."

She settled the tray across his still legs. "Tomorrow's another day. Unless you want oatmeal," she said and stood back, waiting for him to take that first bite of fire. There would be no guessing when he would realize he'd truly bitten off more than he could chew. He'd challenged her to do her worst that morning, and Jeff Carrington was about to learn how bad her worst could be.

"Oh, Emily, you darling lady," he said. "The woman puts the best Cajun chef to shame." He scooped up a fork full and plunged in.

The reaction came quickly and definitively.

"Aah!" Jeff shrieked and searched frantically for something to put out the fire. Something she'd purposely left off the tray. "Water! Milk! Help!"

Hope leaned down and put her nose about two inches from his. "Next time you're tempted to call yourself worthless, Carrington, remember the walls have ears." She lifted the bowl of gumbo off his tray and turned away. "I'll send Emily up with some milk. Notice you put pepper on your own tongue. No one held you down."

"You're dangerous!" Jeff shouted at her retreating back. "And I'm adding attempted murder to the list.

You'll be so deep in a prison they'll have to pump daylight to the lot of you!''

Hope passed Emily Roberts on the stairs. Far from feeling the triumph she'd shown Jeff, she felt awful. "I'll be along with a new plate for him and one for Curt. But I don't feel much like eating tonight."

Emily nodded gravely. "I had to spank him once when he was about five or six for going into a pasture with an untamed stallion. I know how you feel, but you've reminded me that his welfare is more important than his immediate comfort."

"Don't just stand there," they heard Jeff yell, she supposed at Curt. "Get me something to drink."

"And as I'm holding a bit of relief, I'd best run along. The native seems to be restless," Emily quipped and chuckled. "This could actually be good for morale around here. You bellowed, sir," Hope heard the housekeeper say as she entered Jeff's room.

Jeff grabbed the milk like a lifeline. Hope was out of control. He gulped it down and swished it around his burning mouth, hoping all the while that it would quench the fire in his stomach, too. He looked at Emily and tried for his most pitiful expression.

"You have to get rid of her, Mrs. R. She's dangerous. This is a side of her I've never really seen before. You're the only one I can trust now. Help me?"

Mrs. Roberts stood a little straighter, and Jeff felt a rush of satisfaction. She was going to help! He could see her stiffening her resolve. But then she frowned and sat next to him on the bed. Jeff felt his heart sink into despair at the expression on her face. She hadn't worn that look since he was eighteen. But he remembered it well. He was about to get a lecture.

"Now you listen to me, young man. I've kept my mouth shut, but I see that my silence wasn't helping you at all. Hope Taggert *is* helping you." She took his chin in her papery hand and captured his gaze with her own. "That young woman is the best thing to ever happen to you. She cares about you. *You,* not your bank balance. Appreciate it. Appreciate her. She's got more moxie in her little finger than any of those so-called women you've dated over the years. Where are they now, I ask you?"

Jeff looked into the milk glass he still held. He had no answer for that. At least not one she didn't already know. They were off playing at life. He was too much work now.

"Hmm. That's about what I thought," she said of his silent reply. "And that's all I have to say on the subject."

Mrs. Roberts stood and was gone.

Jeff looked at Madden. "I guess you think that whole incident was funny?"

He shrugged. "I think you're a lucky man."

"Lucky? How can you say that? I can't walk. My career is over. My friends have deserted me. I need to pay a stranger to help me take a bath!" He swore. "Oh, that's real lucky."

"Maybe what you need to do is think about all the things you *do* have. The glass half-full instead of half-empty theory. You have Hope and Mrs. Roberts and Manny, who all care about you. You have a roof over your head—and not a shabby one, at that. You have the money to pay someone like me to come in here and help you get better. And you have your health. You're injured but not sick. There are guys your age all over this country dying of crippling diseases. Pardon me if I can't scare up too much sympathy for someone with an eight-figure bank account who had a riding accident when I've worked with kids who never got to walk let alone ride a horse."

Jeff felt ashamed for the first time in years. How had he gotten so selfish? "I don't know where to start," he admitted. "My life's fallen apart and I just don't know how to live this way."

"You do it one day at a time. You learn to rely on God. You become as independent as you can. Maybe that means having a chairlift put on the stairs. Building your upper body strength so you can get in and out and around in your chair. But maybe it means learning to walk again. Maybe..."

"I don't know if I can live life confined to a wheelchair. At least in bed I feel sick."

"But you aren't sick and you may not have to learn how to live that way. One day at a time you'll either get better or you'll learn how to live with not walking. But one thing's for sure, sitting in bed isn't an option. It's giving up."

Curt's words stayed with Jeff long into the night. He hadn't spoken to Hope at all when she came in with more gumbo. She'd played a nasty trick on him, and it hadn't been funny. At least not to him. It hurt to think she might have thought so.

What it *had* done was illustrate to him more clearly than ever how helpless he was. And that she knew how helpless he was.

He hated that she saw him that way, he thought, as he looked at his useless legs. He had nothing to offer her. He'd always felt a woman needed someone she could respect—someone to be strong for her— women's lib or no. And he could no longer be relied upon. He was handicapped. Crippled. Useless. Worthless. And the woman he loved had seen him as just that.

Her presence was torture. Every minute she was here she reminded him of all he'd lost. Since she knew he was no longer the man she needed, she had to be here out of a sense of guilt. Curt was right when he said not trying was giving up. That's all he wanted to do. He wanted to crawl in a hole and pull it in after him, and maybe even be allowed to die in peace. That was the biggest problem with having Hope there. She made him feel alive again. And with life came pain. And that was something he didn't want any more of.

"Good morning." The object of his thoughts spoke as she sailed in with a bright smile on her face and what smelled like a mug of coffee in her hand. She wore crisp indigo jeans and a baby blue sweater. The color of the sweater made her eyes shine like sapphires.

"Did you sleep well?" she asked cheerily. "Curt

said he gave you a massage to relax your muscles at bedtime.''

Jeff tensed. Right. Rub it in. Curt has to put me to bed like a two-year-old. ''Yeah. I slept like a baby,'' he sneered.

Hope put the mug on the bedside table and stepped back. The message in her eyes was clear. She'd obviously thought he'd be more cooperative this morning.

''Uh. I brought you coffee,'' she said, pointing to the rich brown liquid filling the room with its tempting aroma. She opened the terrace curtains then turned to him. ''Curt will be up in a minute,'' she continued, undaunted. ''He's having his first cup at the breakfast bar. If you think you aren't any good before a couple cups, you should see him.''

''You two are certainly getting all nice and cozy in my house.''

Hope's eyebrow climbed her forehead. ''I've known Curtis Madden for years. There's no need for us to get cozy. We went to school together. We've attended the same church since I was twelve when Aunt Meg moved home and started taking me. We were in youth group, summer Bible school and Christian camp together.''

''Hiring him sounds a little like nepotism, don't you think?''

Hope pivoted and stalked toward the door. She turned back when she was halfway there. ''I hired him to help *you!*'' she snapped. ''You are the most ungrateful, spoiled *baby* I've ever had the misfortune to meet.''

Baby? He was a baby, was he? People didn't really see red. It was an old stupid saying. Or so he'd thought. "Get out!" he screamed. But she just stood there. Stood there looking down her superior nose at him, thinking he was a baby. On instinct alone Jeff grabbed the plastic tumbler of water Curt had put next to his bed and threw it at her. The water sloshed all over him, but he didn't care. How dare she rub his nose in his helplessness?

She caught the tumbler easily and threw it at him. It bounced harmlessly to the floor after he let it smack into his chest, just to prove she couldn't hurt him. Down deep he'd known she would catch it and toss it back, but short of pounding his fist into the mattress and really looking juvenile, throwing it at her was his only option. He was, after all, powerless against someone who could storm out and leave him screaming at the air.

Hope's next reaction, however, was so uncharacteristic and unexpected that it took his breath. Tears welled in her big blue eyes, making them sparkle like precious gems. Her chin wobbled when she opened her mouth to speak, and she put her shaking hand up as if to hold off a further attack. And then she ran.

Through the terrace doors a few moments later, Jeff heard Manny call to her, but he couldn't decipher what was said. Nor did he hear a reply. She'd left the draperies open, so he could see her when she got a few hundred feet from the house.

And she was still running.

He felt tears sting his eyes. He hadn't meant to hurt her. Or maybe he had, but it didn't feel anywhere near as good as he'd thought it would. Why were people nasty to one another if it made them feel this awful? How had his parents looked at themselves in the mirror every day?

Jeff kept watching Hope, wanting her to turn and come back so he could apologize, but she kept running. When she reached the pasture fence, he knew she was seeing what he was, his half-wild horse, Mr. March. But that sight meant something different to each of them. She saw in the stallion possibilities for the future ripe for the picking, and he saw his past hopes languishing on the vine.

The stallion he'd raised from a yearling and trained with Hope's help prowled the pasture, clearly unhappy and tense from lack of exercise. Mr. March's head stilled. He turned toward her, then thundered over to where she'd climbed the fence, tossing his head. He paced away restively, then back to her.

Suddenly, recklessly, considering Mr. March's temperament, Hope grabbed the horse's mane and leaped onto his bare back. Jeff's heart pounded as the two flew across the field—a study in fury and freedom. And the heart he'd thought had hardened to stone cracked a little. Because there in that one scene were represented all his wishes and desires—past and present. Lost and yet to be achieved.

Mr. March represented the Olympic dream that had turned to dust, but he also stood for a more distant past when it was Jeff himself riding recklessly across the field, fleeing pain and seeking the joy and the freedom it gave him. Ironic to recognize that what he'd lost in the accident he'd really lost long ago. Joy. And now, as he discovered what he'd truly lost physically, he sat watching the treasure he'd lost that made everything else pale in comparison. For riding away and out of his life was Hope, his heart's desire.

He hadn't meant to hurt her. Just to make her want to go home—for her own good as well as his. Having her near was too painful for him. He would drag her into a world of disabilities where she didn't belong. But he hadn't wanted to make her cry.

"Sticks and stones, Hope. I guess we both forgot," he whispered brokenly.

He'd forgotten how tender her heart was. He'd forgotten how words could injure. Just as he'd forgotten the way it felt to fly with the wind, not to perfect a technique or test his mount's stamina, but to run from pain. To forget hurtful words. And to be free.

Free.

Hope needed to be free. Free of him. Free of the guilt he was sure tied her to him. Only then would she once again be able to go on with her life. But he'd tried cutting her out of his life, and that hadn't done it. She'd moved in and taken over, saying she was going to make him get better. And in trying to get her to give up on him, he'd hurt her. He wasn't strong enough to do that again. She was too precious to him.

Curt walked in, and Jeff looked up, remembering

the things the younger man had said to him the evening before. There was only one way to free her. He had to do what she wanted him to do. He had to cooperate and try to make as much progress as he could. Then she'd see that he didn't need her. What would a few exercises hurt, after all? It would at least relieve some of the boredom.

He'd do as Curt had said. He'd try—at least for today.

Chapter Seven

An hour after leaping on the stallion's back, Hope slowed Mr. March as they approached the rose-brick stable. Manny pushed open the big arch-topped door and waved as she dropped to the ground off Mr. March's back.

The purpose of the wild ride had been simple—to run from the hurt of the nasty scene in Jeff's room. But once she'd managed to block out most of the pain and disillusionment of seeing Jeff become someone she scarcely recognized, she'd realized that he'd been pushing her buttons. And that she'd reacted just as he'd wanted. His rancor had been as much an act to drive her away as her tough stand was an attempt to make him care, and she'd let him get a rise out of her. That had been a mistake—a huge mistake.

But act or not, twice now she'd forced him to be cruel, something he'd never been to another person as long as she'd known him. When they were children, it had always been Cole telling her to bug off and Jeff saying he didn't mind her tagging along. He'd lived his life with cruel, snide remarks flying between his parents and directed at him from both Carringtons. He'd never channeled his pain toward the people in his life. She could never remember him being mean to another person, let alone cruel.

The realization had her wondering if she'd misread the Lord's will. Could her whole approach to helping Jeff be wrong? He wasn't fighting her challenges with that I'll-show-you attitude he'd always had when going after something he wanted. Instead, he was sinking further and further into a mean-spirited kind of existence that was poison to his soul and no life at all for someone like him. She knew Jeff's heart, and he was hurting himself far more than he was hurting her. She had known from the start that her tough love stand could mean that even if she won her battle to get Jeff back on his feet she might lose him in the end. While she didn't believe his claim that he felt only friendship for her, she was very much afraid she may have already pushed him too far and destroyed any possible future for them.

Trying not to show how at odds her thoughts were, Hope turned Mr. March over to one of the handlers for a nice rubdown and washing. It was the one part of being civilized the still half-wild animal loved.

With a heavy heart and the smell of straw and horse sweat filling her nostrils and clinging to her clothes, Hope turned toward the big house on the hill. She was surprised to find Emily Roberts singing happily as she scooted around the kitchen.

"Hope! You're an absolute miracle worker," Emily cried, rushing toward her, a happy grin wreathing her face. "He's coming down for breakfast, and Curt said he's going to start therapy this morning. And it was Jeffrey's idea. It's wonderful. I just know he's going to be fine now."

Surprised by the sudden change, Hope prayed Emily was right.

The clatter of the wheelchair drew her attention and confirmed Emily's claim. Jeff tried twice to negotiate the doorway, but the width of the chair made the task difficult for a beginner. She could see how frustrated he was but didn't know if she should offer help.

"I've got you," Curt said from behind before she decided what to do.

Jeff dropped his fisted hands in his lap. "How's anyone supposed to get around in one of these contraptions?" he complained.

"There are more compact chairs. Once you get stronger, one of those will give you better mobility. After all, you don't need the battery pack or the full arms to keep your seat. Hope, I'll write down some model numbers for the kind I'm talking about and for some additional equipment I think Jeff would benefit from. Could you see about it? And maybe do something about a chairlift on the back stairs?" Curt asked.

Hope nodded and looked at Jeff, but he refused to meet her eyes. The sudden silence in the room was deafening, and the tension between them was clearly uncomfortable to the others. Thankfully, Hope had an excuse to leave.

"Uh, Emily, I was riding and I really need to shower and change. I'll just grab something for myself later."

"You'll do no such thing. No one gets to skip meals in this house as long as I'm around. Go have your shower, and I'll keep your breakfast warm."

Hope blinked and stared at the usually docile Emily. Heavens, she'd created a second monster! Then she heard Jeff snicker and wiped the shocked expression off her face. Instead of protesting, she nodded to Emily, shot Jeff a killing glance and fled his presence for the second time that day.

But there was no fleeing when she returned half an hour later and found Jeff alone in the breakfast room. He was clearly waiting for her. She skidded to a halt two steps into the warm sunny room as he looked up from his nearly empty plate.

"Oh, uh, hi," Jeff said and grimaced. He looked at his plate then at her. His gray eyes were wary and somber. He was dressed in a black sweat suit. He usually looked good in black, but it seemed to exaggerate how pale his skin had grown since February. He stared at her for a long uncomfortable minute, his apology already in his eyes before he said, "I'm sorry for the things I said."

She shrugged. "'S okay."

"No. No, it isn't. I was way out of line."

Hope stared at him. This was the old Jeff. Or at

least a glimpse of him. "And I forgive you," she told him.

He raked his hand through his hair and sighed. "I hate this. I feel so powerless. Helpless. Hopeless. And at the risk of another spiked dinner, worthless. I'm not good for anything anymore."

Hope dropped into a chair near him. "Look, Jeff, God doesn't make junk. Believe that. You've never been worthless a day in your life. That's your father and your coach talking."

"And it turns out they were right, after all. What can I do now?"

Hope was clueless for an answer. She knew what he was talking about, and it wasn't what it would be with most men. What he didn't mean was how did he go about making money? For Jeff that had never been a goal, or a problem, for that matter. He'd followed his father's footsteps into trading on the stock market, but that was only to finance his Olympic aspirations and not for the money's sake. Money was merely a means to an end, not an end result. So what he'd really asked was what was he supposed to replace the dream of a gold medal with? What was he supposed to strive for?

Because Hope had always believed that once he'd achieved his goal of Olympic gold, he would suddenly find his life empty, she had an answer ready. And it was an answer he wouldn't want to hear. She put her hand over his where it lay fisted on the table between them. "Seek the Lord, Jeff. He knows what you need to do. Ask Him."

Jeff shook his head. "You know how I feel about all that hocus-pocus."

Hope rolled her eyes. "I have never said faith was magic. You don't even try to understand."

"No. I don't. Because I don't believe it. Come on, Hope. What kind of merciful God would let me get crippled this way? And what about my parents? And yours? Mine are dead. Your mother was killed by a crazed horse with your father and brother watching. Your father's never recovered. Neither has Cole. It's torn your family apart for years. And your aunt Meg? She's still grieving for a guy who went off to war and never came home."

"Because we have free will. And we make mistakes. You were hurt because I was careless." She held up her hand to stop his protest. "No. I missed a badly worn girth. I still can't believe I did something so stupid, but I did it. I finally know how my father felt all those years ago for not listening to Cole about that horse. But he didn't listen, did he? It was his choice to ignore his son's protests in the interest of getting Cole back in the saddle after the horse threw him. Unfortunately Dad set the incident that killed my mother into motion.

"Another person who was wrong was my mother. She didn't have to step in between Cole and Dad that day. She didn't have to prove the horse was safe.

"Then there's Cole," she continued, ticking off the people he'd cited. "Cole could have reached out to my father sometime in the last fourteen years. And vice versa. Your parents didn't have to leave that party with a friend who'd been drinking and let him drive.

"And Aunt Meg could have looked for love again after her fiancé was killed in Vietnam. She chose to stay alone."

Hope covered his hand again. "All those things happened because we have free will. Because God gave us free will. What we do with our free will can bring joy or heartache into our lives or the lives of others."

Jeff was shaking his head. "I'm not buying it. You're just rationalizing."

"You are so stubborn!"

He pulled his hand from hers. "No more so than you!"

They looked at each other. It was such a typical debate between them. The kind she missed. He smiled. She chuckled.

"Some things never change, do they?" he asked, still smiling.

"No. They don't," she replied and reached for what she assumed was the list of exercise equipment Curt had promised to leave for her.

Jeff practically snatched it out of her hand.

"Isn't that the list Curt left for me?"

"I don't need all this."

"You heard Curt. He says you do."

"I'm paying him enough. He can just improvise and earn his salary."

Hope crossed her arms. "He'll earn his salary by getting you on the road to recovery. What's the real problem here? You aren't lazy, Jeff. So it isn't the work involved. You've never been cheap or stingy, so it isn't the money that stuff will cost. What are you afraid of?''

"I'm not afraid! I—I…" He slapped the list down between them. "Fine. Go spend my money. You're right. I don't care.''

Hope stood and smiled, then, on impulse, she leaned down and kissed his cheek. "Thanks. I will. How about we go see how that exercise room is coming?''

Jeff took a deep breath. Then fought to take another. Therapy? Why not just call it what is was?

Torture.

The inquisition.

He took another breath. Or tried. But the bunching muscles in his back and legs tightened, robbing him of what felt like his last thread of sanity. For the first time in his entire life, Jeffrey Carrington let someone else know he was in pain. He let out a howl loud enough to wake the dead.

And Curt Madden.

The supposedly hard-to-wake, four-cup-a-jump-start therapist arrived wide awake at his side in a nanosecond. "Spasms?'' Madden asked.

In the grip of an even worse cramp than the previous one, Jeff managed to nod, then he buried his face in his pillow, letting it absorb the cold sweat and his humiliating tears. Then breathing seemed to lose its involuntary status. Jeff found himself fighting to suck air in around the pain and expel it to make room for the next breath. Then he felt Madden's hands on his back and tensed even more.

"Try to relax," Curt ordered. "Do you want medication?"

"Anything. My abs are starting to cramp now. I'm going to get sick. Do something. Lethal injection couldn't be worse than this."

Somehow the RN managed to get the medication into him, and Jeff managed to keep it down. He couldn't remember when his mind started to clear of the excruciating agony that had awakened him out of the depth of sleep. Though it was now on a level he could handle, Jeff was still in considerable pain. Almost on cue, embarrassment crept into its place as Curt manipulated the protesting muscles.

"Try to relax and go with the pain. Let it wash over you like a wave but try not to react to it. Let sleep come back and..."

Jeff closed his eyes and listened to the hypnotic rhythm of Curt's voice. It reminded him of the way Hope's voice sounded when she was working with a particularly skittish horse. Calm. Reassuring. Restful. A voice you could trust, he thought some minutes later as he slipped into exhausted sleep.

The next thing he knew, a cool breeze flowed across his skin and soft sunlight kissed the air. He was still facedown on the bed. And it was morning. He'd made it through the night.

Jeff didn't know how he was going to face therapy again that day knowing what the increased activity would do to him in the night. He'd noticed it early on. The more they moved him around for tests in the hospital, the worse his muscles had cramped in the night. The therapy wasn't worth it. Why couldn't they leave him alone?

He opened his eyes and saw Hope sitting on the floor by his bed. She wore a soft peach sweater and a matching skirt that draped over bent knees and flowed onto the floor covering all but the tips of her shoes. Her head rested on her arms which were wrapped around her upraised knees. Her position didn't look very comfortable.

Guilt struck him.

He was about to disappoint her, but it couldn't be helped. This wasn't going to work. He'd rather die than suffer the shame again of screaming out in the night. He was thankful that with Hope sleeping in the homestead house, she couldn't have heard him, but Curt had, and, no doubt, Mrs. R.

Hope must have felt him watching her because her eyes flew open and she blushed. "Oh. You're awake! Hi."

"Ditto," he replied, his voice rough as sandpaper. Probably from that guttural scream he'd let out when the spasms had awakened him to a world of darkness and pain.

He tried to clear his throat. "Where's super nurse this morning?" he asked.

"Curt should be right back. They needed him to check out the equipment that's being delivered. And there's a mirror installer down there putting mirrors on a couple walls. I heard you had a bad night.''

"You could say that.''

"I'm sorry. Curt was able to help you, though. Right?''

With some difficulty, Jeff rolled over then pulled himself up in the bed while he considered how to answer her question without giving away too much about the night before. "Sure,'' he said with a careless shrug. "He beat the pain into submission after about an hour.''

"I'd heard he was good at what he does. That's why I wanted him here to help you. You don't have any problem with moving out of this room for a while, do you?''

Was she trying to keep him constantly off balance? "Why would I move out? This has always been my room.''

"Because Curt thought the ground floor of the guest wing would be better for you two. He's setting up an exercise room in a room near the hot tub and whirlpool. He also thought since there are ground-floor bedrooms in the guest wing you could both move into a couple of them, and we could avoid the expense and mess of the chairlift on the back stairs.''

Jeff cleared his throat again and looked away. "Forget it. He's wasting his time, Hope. So are you. The more I try, the worse I am. Look at last night.''

"It's my business how I spend my time, and Curt's being paid for his. And before you say it's your money that's being wasted, you know you don't care.

Try to be positive. Maybe the pain will get better.
Maybe you'll get better. Can you risk not trying? Really?''

Jeff stared at her earnest face. It was the face he
longed to kiss. The face that always faded away before their lips met in his dreams. Maybe he could
hang in there for a little while just to show her that
he had tried but that it was hopeless. Then she'd have
to give up and go home to her family and leave him
to his broken life and his even more painfully broken
heart.

That afternoon Jeff rolled into the room Hope and
Curt had set aside as his bedroom and looked around
with a disgusted sigh. Like many of the rooms in the
house, it was eternally white and stark. All the com-
forts of home, Jeff thought sarcastically. It was even
more impersonal than his hospital room had been. His
mother would have loved it.

He may as well have gone to that rehab the doctors
had tried to stick him in. He'd lost just as much control over his life here as he would have in an impersonal institution. Next thing they'd probably do was
hand him a schedule to live by. At least at the rehab
some decorator would have carefully chosen colors to
cheer the poor invalid.

This, Hope had told him, was all for his benefit.
She probably believed it, too. Hope would never do
anything to hurt him, but it was a little hard to feel
grateful. It didn't seem to matter to anyone that he

wanted his space. His own bed. His own furniture. His own carefully painted walls surrounding him.

He was to sleep in a hospital bed which, though he hated to admit it, would probably make him a lot more comfortable than his own bed. There was a trapeze bar suspended by a frame that hung over the bed to help him sit up, turn over and get in the chair. The mattress was topped with an air bladder like the one in the hospital. It was made up with institutional looking sheets. White, of course. But comfortable and convenient though it might be, it was still the bed of a cripple. He wouldn't even be able to pretend to be normal in bed anymore.

"So, what do you think?" Hope asked from behind him.

Jeff refused to looked at her. She sounded nervous. He was sure she was perceptive enough of his moods to know that this change wasn't one he was happy with. And he knew she wasn't trying to hurt him. But even her limited presence in his life did that. Why couldn't she go home and leave him alone?

"Does my opinion matter?" he snapped.

He had the luxury of not seeing her face and was grateful when he heard the hurt in her answer. "This is all for your own good, Jeff. Of course your opinion matters."

"Then tell me. Did you sterilize the walls, too? It's about as personal! I like my room. It was the one thing I was allowed to pick when my father had this mausoleum built. I was only three, but I remember walking from room to room and trying to decide which one was mine. I remember it seemed impossible to choose because it all looked the same. Then I walked into my room. Maybe it was the terrace that looked out over the pastures. Or the tree that used to be outside the window. It was summer and the tree was bright green against the white walls. It was the first color I'd seen since I arrived. I don't know for sure what it was, but the room felt like home.''

Her heart hitched at the sadness in his voice. "I'm sorry. This is only temporary. Pretty soon you'll be able to walk into your room and feel at home again.''

He wheeled around to face her. "And what if all your optimism is off the mark?''

"Then we'll put in the chairlift and you can move back up there. Either way, this is just temporary. I promise.''

Jeff looked away. He hated seeing her hurting, and almost as much, he hated the guilt he heard in her voice. It reminded him that guilt was the only reason she was here, now that he'd told her there was no future for them.

"Tell you what,'' Hope said after a few silent moments. "Suppose I call in some men to move the armoire and bureau down here. And maybe hanging some of your paintings would make it feel less impersonal. If you still hate it too much, we'll get an elevator chairlift put in and move you back upstairs. How does that sound?'' she asked.

In the interest of cooperation, maybe he could stand the white walls with his paintings hanging and his things around him. At least this way there wouldn't be all the problems with getting him up to his room, and if he really did hate it he could still have the elevator installed.

"All right. But only if I decide I want to stay down here. Deal?"

She smiled, and the room brightened as surely as if the sun had suddenly risen right there. "Deal. I should have thought of transferring your stuff with you. I'm sorry. I'll get right on it."

Hope pivoted and rushed out before he recovered from the effects of that smile. He hadn't told her he'd once again decided to give up on the idea of therapy. Mrs. Roberts seemed to understand that the pain it caused was too unbearable. Now he wasn't sure he *could* tell Hope. If he stopped trying to work with Curt, he'd never set her free. And much as he wanted to keep her with him forever, he knew he couldn't tie her to him the way he was—half a man.

"Did you convince him to keep working at it?" Curt asked as Hope entered the kitchen. Emily turned anxious eyes toward her, as well.

Hope sat and grabbed one of Emily's cookies. "He just complained about the room." She chuckled. "Actually he demanded to know if we'd sterilized the walls. It's obvious his tastes don't run parallel to his mother's." She told them about the compromise she and Jeff had reached over the room.

"But he didn't tell you he didn't want to do his therapy because of last night?" Emily took a seat at

the table with Hope and Curt. "He seemed so determined to quit earlier."

"I'm afraid Jeff feels his life isn't his to control
any more," Curt added. "And screaming last night
bothered him a lot."

Hope agreed. "Jeff's always been about control. I
guess losing control enough to scream the way he did
would have felt like the ultimate loss of control. I've
always thought that's why he enjoyed riding and why
he took on that half-wild animal out there in the pasture. That way he could control the seemingly uncon-
trollable. It's probably the same with his investments
and the breeding program."

"At least he didn't give up again," Emily said, the
worry clearing from her lined face.

"He must have rethought his decision after the pain
faded," Hope ventured.

"It's more likely that he doesn't want to disappoint
you, dear," Emily replied.

Curt nodded his agreement.

Hope couldn't deny or confirm it, so she shrugged
and stood. "Well, it's time this girl hits the books.
Do me a favor, drag me out of there for lunch before
I OD on finance. This really isn't my forte but there's
not much left to do around the stables today, and from
the depth of the mail on that desk, I'd say my work's
cut out for me."

Making her way to Jeff's office, Hope thought of
the room where Jeff used to work. The walls, lined
with shelf after shelf of books both new and old, gave
her the same warm feeling her office at Laurel Glen

did. She was tempted to build a fire in the fireplace but knew she'd probably fall asleep. She hadn't let Jeff know but she'd been in the kitchen in the early morning hours heating some milk to help her sleep when Jeff screamed. Only knowing that he wouldn't want her there had kept her out of his room. But she'd stood in the hall until Curt's massage and the drugs let him rest comfortably.

It was easy to see why he'd gotten so discouraged and why it would be such a temptation to quit trying. If her presence kept him working toward a goal, even if that goal was not disappointing her, she'd stay till she was old and gray, Hope thought, and settled behind the big desk.

She glanced at the stack of bills and financial statements she'd sorted into piles and groaned. There were, however, plenty of other reasons for her to stay. Jeff apparently hadn't been taking care of the household's finances, the stable feed bills or his stocks since the accident. Right now, working at his therapy would be all he could handle, so she would have to fill in for him as best she could.

Hope wished she'd paid more attention in her finance classes. She'd been able to figure out the discrepancies Billy Dever had caused in Emily's petty cash account, and with care yesterday she'd balanced Jeff's several checking accounts. She was perfectly able to write checks to pay utility, grocery and feed bills, and she did that first. Two hours later all bills were paid and she'd mastered the payroll software.

Since the next day was Friday and payday at Lavender Hill, she wrote those checks, as well.

She had lunch then, for the rest of the afternoon, answered inquiries about stud fees and possible purchases of Lavender Hill's yearlings. Then she sat, staring at the last pile. What did she do with all this stuff about the stock market? The whole concept escaped her, from how to trade stocks right down to what good it was in the first place. Hope was never so grateful as when she heard Emily's sweet grandmotherly voice accompany a knock on the door. Saved by dinner!

Chapter Eight

Jeff crossed his arms and shot Hope and Curt a mutinous stare. "I said I'm on strike! For one solid month all I've done is what you two tell me to do. Including taking naps! I'm sick of it."

"Can you honestly sit there and tell me you're not doing better?" Curt asked.

"The operative word is *sit!*"

"Jeff," Hope cajoled, "you knew going in it would take a while. You lost your first month and a lot of ground with it. First you had to get back to square one. But as Curt said, you're better. The cramps are coming less and less. You sleep for less time during those horrible naps, but you do sleep. You can get yourself into your chair and into the tub and back out. You've lost all the fat you put on and gained muscle. You're moving forward now."

"I'm *rolling* forward," he retorted. And that was the real problem. He'd wanted to believe that this wasn't all there was going to be in his life. He'd begun to believe Curt could really help him. He'd begun to believe in miracles. Then last night he'd dreamed of dancing with Hope in his arms, but when he'd awakened this morning, he'd found himself still unable to stand. It was a bitter pill to swallow to have to sit there and look up into her eyes when she should have been gazing up into his.

At the time of the accident, he'd thought he might be in love with her, and he'd wanted to explore the possibility. But now, when he couldn't, he knew there was no speculation about it. It was a simple fact. He loved her. And he would lose her.

The sooner the better.

A quick pain was better than this drawn-out cycle of agony—dreams of a glowing future in the night and the realization of the truth as day dawned.

"Why don't you both go home and leave me in peace? Go torture someone you can help," he said to Curt, then pinned Hope with a virulent look. "Go home and train horses and stop trying to train me. Why are you here, anyway? I don't need either of you. I can take care of myself for the most part now. I'll hire someone else to help me with what I can't do alone."

Jeff looked away from the wounded expression on Hope's face. He'd hurt her. He tried to make himself ignore the deep shame that came over him, but he couldn't. "I'm sorry," he said, not even waiting for Hope's response.

"Curt, would you leave us alone for a few

minutes?'' Hope asked. When Curt nodded and left after a long assessing look at both of them, Hope silently moved a chair in front of Jeff and sat facing him. ''Want to talk about it?'' she asked calmly. Kindly.

Jeff blinked. She was supposed to be angry. She was supposed to leave. He deserved an irate set down, not sweet understanding. ''There's nothing to talk about. I'm an ungrateful louse who doesn't deserve a friend like you.''

She shook her head. ''Not good enough. Something happened between last night and this morning. What has you so discouraged today?''

Jeff wondered how she knew him so well and fought the urge to reach out and touch her. It was the same every time she was near. He looked away—and straight into his own face reflected in the mirrored wall of the exercise room.

He turned his head, unable to look at himself. He wanted her here as much if not more than he wanted her to leave. And it shamed him almost as much as hurting her had. To cover his nearly overwhelming need and to distract himself from her nearness, Jeff decided to admit to half the truth.

''I had a dream that I could walk. Then I woke up and I couldn't. Nothing mysterious. Just a cold dip in life's pool of miserable reality.''

Hope reached out and gripped his hand where it lay fisted on his useless legs. ''But that's only the reality of the moment,'' she told him, her voice rife with deep conviction. ''It's not the reality of the future. The future is fluid. Always moving. Always changing and shifting. Your situation can turn around at any time."

Jeff looked into her beautiful eyes and knew the answer to his next question even before he asked it. The truth of her incredible faith in him was there in the depths of those eyes he loved so much. But there was something else there, too, and it hurt. "Do you really believe that, or is it your guilt talking? You know, wishful thinking to get you off the hook? I told you I don't blame you for the accident. I should have checked my own tack."

Hope shook her head. "No. I made the mistake. I am guilty. I feel guilty. There's no point denying it. But I also really believe you'll walk again."

Jeff closed his eyes and dropped his head back, then, taking a deep breath and drawing in her unique scent, he gazed at her again, his heart as heavy with the weight of her belief in him as his body was with his need of her. "You have more faith in me than I deserve."

"You don't give yourself enough credit," Hope said as she smiled and stood. "You never have. I wish you could forget every negative word you heard about yourself from your parents."

"Mother wasn't so bad. At least she was too busy with committees and her tennis to have much time left for criticism. Unfortunately, my father was such a genius that he only had to spend half his days making his fortune. That left him the rest of the time for me and all my faults."

Hope looked into his eyes. "I wish you could see what I see in you. And I wish you knew what I know. You have another Father, Jeff, and He wouldn't see anything but His perfect child if you'd put your faith in His Son."

Jeff blew a sharp breath through his lips. "You never give up, do you?"

"Wouldn't I be an awfully selfish person if I kept His good news to myself when it's given me such joy and peace of mind? I want you to share in His joy, Jeff. He could give you that and so much more."

Jeff had to admit, even if just to himself, that he'd never really looked at it in that way. He'd always thought she wanted to drag him to church and make his life as boring as hers. A misery-likes-company sort of scenario.

"You know what you need?" Hope continued. "You need a day off and a change of scene. We need to get you out and about in the world again."

Jeff's stomach turned to rock. "No. I'm fine. I don't need to get out. I don't want to get out. I like it here just fine."

"You can't stay cooped up here. Pretty soon you won't be able to face going off the property. My great-aunt was like that, and she didn't go out of her house for years before her death."

"I'm not your aunt." Jeff gritted his teeth. He was sick to death of feeling like a weakling around her. "I don't want people pointing at me and wondering what happened to me. I don't want to look *up* at a bunch of strangers from a chair, or sit in the handicapped section at the movies, or have waiters trying to figure out where to stick me so I won't be in their way. Don't tell me it won't happen because I've seen it happening to other people. I was probably one of the insensitive clods gawking.''

"Jeff—"

"No! I don't want to go anywhere. Drop it!" he snarled and pivoted the chair so he could stare out the window. Seconds later he heard her withdraw quietly from the room. Hands fisted, Jeff pounded again and again on his useless legs, satisfied that at least they still felt pain.

When a week had passed with no indication that Jeff was ready to face the world, Hope decided to talk about it with Curt. She found him seated at the wrought-iron table on the stone patio off the breakfast room. He'd begun to brave the cool spring air to sit with his coffee, reading the Word before breakfast.

After bringing up the subject of Jeff's increasing avoidance of the outside world, she asked, "Do you think I should just force him to go somewhere?"

While Curt considered her question, Hope said a quick prayer that Curt would have a better suggestion. Even though Jeff was improving physically, she knew that every time she pushed him she tested the love she prayed he still felt for her. The possibility that he'd meant what he'd said that day when he called her pathetic haunted her sleep.

Hope's heart fell when Curt shook his head. "I doubt that would do more than make him hopping mad along with making him feel he's lost control of another aspect of his life. I don't think it's a good idea, but I confess I don't have another one. Maybe we should just let it ride a while longer.''

Hope frowned and gazed over the evenly mowed fields that by summer would be tall with alfalfa. The fields were crisscrossed with sparkling white fences, as they had been when Jeff's grandfather ran Lavender Hill as a horse farm. Along the knee-high stone wall that surrounded the terrace, lined up like soldiers awaiting battle, sat several verdigris planters resplendent with purple and yellow crocuses. Rather than cheer her, the beautiful scene saddened her. The world was bursting with life and change, and Jeff was missing it all.

There had to be a way to get him out and about without driving a wedge between them, she thought. But what if she did get him out and his worst fears came true? What if people did stare? What if someone openly showed pity for him?

The only safe place she could think to take him was her church. She was sure the people at the Tabernacle would accept him as her friend and take him at face value. Of course, getting Jeff to go to a church service would be even harder than getting him to go to a dinner or movie.

Obviously seeing her distress, Curt took her hand and gave it a comforting squeeze. ''Hope, he's not going to agree yet. And you can't force the man to do everything you want.''

Hope sighed. "I know. I wouldn't love him if I could."

"Let's give it to the Lord and ask Him to show us the way."

Nodding, Hope joined hands with Curt and closed her eyes as he prayed for guidance and patience with Jeff. Curt's prayers for patience were less desperate these days than they once had been. It was proof positive that Jeff's attitude toward therapy had improved as much as his muscle tone. She tried to be grateful, but she wanted so much more for him than to be called cooperative by two of the few people in his life.

"Hey, you two," Emily called out the back door. "Breakfast in a few minutes. I've called Jeff."

"Thanks, Mrs. R," Curt called and let go of Hope's hand, his prayer concluded. "You better be ready for a hungry man. I could eat a horse this morning."

"Ouch, Madden. I've told you that's not an expression to use around horse people," Jeff called, laughter in his voice. He sat behind Emily in the doorway.

Curt chuckled. "With all the developments going up and all the executives moving in along the main roads, I keep forgetting that there are still so many horse farms out here on the side roads."

"That's sad, Madden. Look out there. You're living on a horse farm. And over yonder is Laurel Glen, one of the biggest in the state!"

With Jeff's words, Hope's thoughts winged their

way to Laurel Glen. She was still too tied to her home to forget the reality of what all those starter castles sprouting up meant financially for her father and the farm that had been in the Taggert family for centuries. She turned and looked toward home.

"If we can't find a way to hold the line against rising property taxes, this part of Chester County is going to be as built up as the northern part of the county," she mused sadly.

"Is Laurel Glen having problems?" Jeff asked from behind her. She'd missed the sound of the wheels in her musings and turned to face him.

How could she tell him that rumor about his accident had caused her father more setbacks than the rising taxes that plagued nearly every farm in the county? Especially when the rumors were true. He *had* been crippled by a careless worker and poorly maintained tack. Her carelessness. Her father's tack. Each mistake had been inconsistent with both of them. But the result was still Jeff in a wheelchair and her at Lavender Hill searching for ways to help him venture into the world.

The snap of Jeff's fingers in front of her face jolted Hope to the matter at hand. "Hey, space cadet, I'm still waiting. Is your dad in trouble?" he asked when her eyes locked with his.

She looked away and grimaced. "Let's just say profits are down." Way down. And she felt guilty about that, as well. The farm's downhill slide had begun with her mistake. Should she be there helping? Was her insistence on helping Jeff dishonoring her father? He was probably doing the job of two, and without her there, Aunt Meg was stuck refereeing between Cole and Ross.

Hope told herself that part of the situation had been caused by her father's decisions and by his stubbornness. Unfortunately, that didn't ease her guilt a whit. She kept giving it to the Lord, along with her guilt over Jeff's injuries, but both loads of guilt kept coming back. That had never happened to her before when she'd asked Him to carry a burden for her. She needed to talk to Pastor Jim about it. Maybe he could figure out what she was doing wrong.

"Ross should get the other farm and stable owners together to see that their tax structure..."

Hope stared at Jeff, letting his words and ideas fly over her head like brilliantly crafted paper airplanes. He had such a fine mind, and she had a feeling he also had every bit of his father's financial genius.

"Would you talk to my father about all that?" she asked, thinking that maybe that was a way to show her father how much substance there was to Jeff. "I'm afraid having their wills in order and working like men possessed are the limits of Taggert family financial planning. It was about all my grandfather did, and I'll bet that's all Dad's done."

Jeff shook his head. "He'd never listen to me."

Hope smiled. "Then we'll have to work on that, won't we?"

"Are you two going to come in and eat this before it gets cold?" Emily called.

"Uh-oh. We better get in there," Jeff joked. "Mrs.

R on the warpath isn't a pretty sight. I'm telling you, you created a monster.''

"You just have your nose out of joint because you can't wrap her around your little finger anymore."

"I've noticed a certain amount of steel in her spine toward you these days. Like when you try to skip meals. You get away with less than I do.'' He smiled that smile she saw rarely lately, and her heart turned over.

There was something about Jeff that she had learned over the years. It was a simple truth that he'd never understood his power over women. He used it unconsciously and never really knew what he did that attracted them. It was that unconscious artlessness that she'd fallen in love with first.

Since his accident, he'd obviously tried to analyze what used to have women flocking to his side and giving him his way. He'd tried arrogance. Tried carelessness. Even tried looking pathetic. But none of those things had anything to do with his real charm.

His charm was in the air of naïveté his smile showed. It gave away his obliviousness to the very thing women couldn't resist. He projected that charm by the boatload with his hopeful smile and the mischief glimmering in his eyes.

And that gave her a sudden brilliant idea. *Let this be from you, Lord,* she prayed. *Please don't let me make a mistake and destroy whatever Jeff feels for me.*

They had all discussed Jeff's needs and what he had to learn to do on his own in case he never walked

again. At first Hope hadn't wanted Curt to spend time
on anything but helping him walk. It smacked of giving up. But Curt Madden knew his stuff, so she'd
backed off. Next on the agenda was for Jeff to learn
to survive in the kitchen. But Curt hadn't yet told Jeff
that today was the day they'd start working in Emily's
domain. And Jeff hadn't a clue how to manipulate
Emily these days because he was trying too hard and
she saw right through his efforts.

Hope arched an eyebrow and smirked at him.

"What's that look about?" he demanded, taking
up Hope's challenge as if on cue.

"She's just fussing over my eating habits. She
feeds me wherever she can find me. But who was it
who had to come to the lunch table yesterday when
he wanted to eat in the whirlpool? It's your number
Emily's got." She could almost see that wonderful
competitive streak rise in him.

"At breakfast we'll see who she pays more attention to," Jeff challenged.

Hope added another smirk, just to egg him on.
"Okay, hotshot. If she pays more attention to you
than me, I have to do something you want me to do.
And the same goes for you."

"Anything?" he asked with a strange gleam in his
eyes.

Hope glared, wondering what was going on in his
mind. "Anything as long it isn't immoral or dangerous," she added, to be certain all her bases were covered.

Jeff nodded and pivoted the chair toward the breakfast room door, and she sailed in behind him, dropping into one of the fruitwood chairs. Sunshine glinted though the crisp curtains and shone on the copper sugar bowl and creamer on the table. She loved this room. The hominess of it. Like Jeff's room—his real room upstairs—the kitchen and breakfast nook area no longer suffered the cold brush of his mother's stark taste. This was one of the few rooms Jeff had bothered to redecorate after her death.

"I have a lot on my list for today, Emily. I really just want coffee," Hope said.

"You will do no such thing!"

"Then would you mind if I ate in the study?"

"Oh, not at all dear," Emily replied with a sweet smile. "I'll just fix you up a nice tray."

Hope sent a smirk Jeff's way as Emily fussed. Trying to cause as little work for her as possible, Hope got out the tray and grabbed a place setting of flatware off the table.

As the older woman set a plate on the tray, Jeff said, "You know, that looks like a good idea. Would you bring mine into my room?"

"No, I will not. You just get yourself right up to that table and eat like a gentleman. Honestly, as if a body hasn't got more to do than wait on you hand and foot."

Jeff stared at Emily in amazement, then he looked toward Hope, his eyes narrowed. "You set me up."

Hope shook her head. "You set yourself up, pal. We leave at six-thirty."

"Leave?"

"We're going out tonight. Dress casual. Or are you going to welsh on our bet?"

A muscle in his jaw pulsed as he gritted his teeth. "I'll be ready."

Jeff pushed his way toward the door to the hall feeling like a man on his way to his own execution. He stopped and glanced at his watch. Six twenty-five. At least he was right on time. Hope thought she was going to teach him something about human nature tonight, but it was Hope who was in for the lesson. Unfortunately, it would mean his own humiliation.

Muscles knotting and dinner lying like a rock in his nervous stomach, Jeff forced himself to roll forward. Hope and Curt stood in the foyer. "Coming to help or watch?" he asked Madden.

Curt stepped forward. "Jeff, if you don't want to go—"

"No, I don't want to go, but I let her push me and I lost. If I was stupid enough to fall into her trap, then I guess I ought to be man enough to pay the piper."

"Jeff—" Hope began.

"I don't want or need your backpedaling," he cut in. "Let's get this over with. I assume the answer to my earlier question was help," he told Madden. "So how do we go about getting the invalid into the car?"

"It's a van and it's equipped with a chairlift," Hope told him.

"Think of everything, don't you?" he grumbled.

It took a little longer than he liked, but Jeff soon

found himself ensconced inside the van. Curt climbed behind the wheel and Hope climbed in next to him.

"So, where are we going?" Jeff asked.

"The Tabernacle."

Incredulous, he stared at her for a long moment. Jeff could have sworn he felt his blood pressure skyrocket. She wouldn't! "I am not going to your church. You know how I feel about that!"

"You said anything. If you had won, what were you going to ask me to do?"

He felt like a volcano overdue to blow. She was too much! "I was going to make you go home," he snapped.

"And I want you to go out. No one at the Tabernacle will stare or point or ask embarrassing questions. I know these people. They're good and decent and kind. This will be the perfect place for you to start getting out into the world again. I'm not demanding you listen to Pastor Dillon. Sit and twiddle your thumbs. I don't care."

"Take me home," he demanded.

"You promised! What are you afraid of?"

Jeff gritted his teeth. Why did she always make him feel like a coward? "I'm not afraid! Fine. I'll go to your stupid church."

Chapter Nine

It didn't take nearly enough time to get to the church, Hope thought. Jeff was still silently brooding. The sight of the big converted barn usually washed a sense of peace over her. Not so tonight. She looked at Jeff, his expression forbidding as the lift carried him to the ground and he sank from her view. Her nervous stomach flipped. She thought he'd relax a little on the ride. Lose the scowl, at least.

"Maybe we should leave," she whispered to Curt Madden as Jeff rolled forward and off the lift a few seconds later.

"Not on your life," Curt told her as he closed and locked her door. "He's here, and right now, I don't care to tempt fate by suggesting that this is too much for him. Jeff's lost enough pride."

"That's my fault. I think he hates me to see him fail."

Curt nodded. "Yeah. He does. But that's also an

advantage because he works harder to keep you from seeing him fall flat on his face.''

"Are you two going to stand there and whisper about me all night or are we going to get this over with?" Jeff snarled.

"Sorry," Curt said. "You think you can handle getting in yourself? I'm on stage tonight."

"Go. I'll handle it," he told Curt, then looked at the rustic building. "This isn't the church you used to go to. I thought you said you've known Curt since you two were kids."

"This isn't where we met. By coincidence we both come here now. Aunt Meg found the Tabernacle just after they started meeting at the firehouse. Curt was already a member with his parents."

"What kind of crazy church meets in a firehouse then moves to a barn?"

"It's my kind of church." Hope grinned. The Tabernacle was a little unconventional. That's why she loved it. "You go in the front door and the love of the Lord is just in there. Pastor Jim and some of the original members helped rebuild the building from the framing out with their own two hands. He says he just couldn't tear it down even though that was the original plan. That smaller building next to the barn is for our youth ministry. Pastor Jim moved it up here from the back of the property a couple years ago. He did the finish work on it almost single-handedly. That was just before he remarried his wife."

"Your pastor was divorced?"

After a chuckle, she added, "He's also recovering alcoholic. The church actually started as an Alcoholics Anonymous Bible study. He still runs AA meetings out of the church. Quite a colorful bunch around here. We're all sinners, Jeff. No one considers themself better than anyone else at the Tabernacle. If you'd give us a chance, you might find you even like us."

Jeff looked at her, his expression inscrutable. "I like you just fine. It's all the holier-than-thou strangers in there that I'm not too sure of." He looked at himself. "You said dress casual. Are you sure I don't clash with the chair or their dress code?"

Hope spread her arms and turned so he could inspect her denim skirt and casual top. "Does it look as if I dressed up? Believe me, in chinos and a golf shirt you're overdressed, if anything. And how could black clash with a mostly black chair?"

Jeff didn't crack a smile but pivoted and pushed toward the ramp and the front doors. He stopped and pointed down the hill at the new construction toward the back of the property. "What's that?"

"A house for Pastor Jim and his family. It still needs a lot of work. Since his wife just found out she's expecting their second child, we're going to be working pretty hard to get it done now that spring's here."

"Evening, Hope," Pastor Jim Dillon called as they approached the front door. A tall, dark and handsome James Bond look-alike, he reached out and shook Jeff's hand. "A new face," the pastor said.

"Jeff Carrington. Pastor Jim Dillon," she said, introducing the men.

Jim Dillon was probably the same height as Jeff, but he somehow managed to shake Jeff's hand while not seeming to stoop to do it. "Welcome," the young pastor said. "It's always nice to see someone new."

"Well, don't get used to seeing me. She all but twisted my arm to get me here," Jeff growled.

Hope felt her face flame.

Pastor Jim chuckled. "Kidnapped another one, did you, Hope? Well, don't worry, Jeff. She's harmless most of the time, and I'm sure that she'll take you back where she found you after I get a shot at boring you for an hour or so." He looked past them and waved as a van pulled into a nearby parking spot. "You two may want to move to a safe place. Here comes the Osborne tribe."

Hope looked across the parking lot and smiled. "Come on. He's not kidding. Five kids, two parents and two grandmothers are about to pour out of that van."

They moved on, and Jeff, a bit less angry but still sullen, kept his eyes on the floor ahead of him. Hope sighed and silently prayed that the message would touch him.

As they entered the sanctuary, the praise and worship team, including Curt on bass, started playing. One of the ushers smoothly removed a chair as Hope moved into a row. "I'll just get this thing out of your way," he said to Jeff with a sheepish smile, as if it were the seat that was out of place and not Jeff's chair. A fervent prayer that hearts would be touched by the study that night followed the first song.

Pastor Jim, who taught verse by verse through each book of the Bible, was in Exodus that night. "You know when I read this section of Exodus I start to feel really sorry for poor old Moses," he began. "You have to look at what this guy's been through up to this point and remember that he's no spring chicken. This is an eighty-year-old guy who's tromping around in the desert. And these Israelites are a tough bunch to play to. He must be exhausted by this time.

"I mean, here he is—God's spokesman back in Egypt. He helped God get the Chosen People out of there after hundreds of years of slavery. He was the instrument of God's wrath and called down all sorts of privation on the people of Egypt. Then when they were being chased, he parted the Red Sea and drowned the army pursuing them.

"Remember when the Israelites were thirsty and they came to poor old Moses to complain? He cried out to the Lord for them, and the Lord answered by turning the waters of Marah sweet so they could drink. Then they came to him grousing because they were hungry. So God sent them manna.

"Now how hard is this? Go to sleep, wake up and pick up the food that's laying all over the ground. They're told to take only what they could eat in one day. For a while it was okay. They had ba-manna bread. Manna-cotti. Marsh-mannas. But did this bunch stay content? Nope, some of them had to test God and keep more than they could eat in a day.''

Hope was gratified to see Jeff relax enough to laugh with the rest of the congregation.

''I know what you're all thinking,'' Pastor Jim went on. ''If God was doing miracles like that in my life, I'd honor Him. I'd trust Him. I'd take what He gave and be happy for it. But would you? How many of us have been given everything we need to live and we're still not happy? How many of us are out there Monday through Saturday trying to finagle a way to get more? And how many of us get what we're after only to find that it's all wrong for us, that it makes us miserable?

''How about those of us who really do need something? Do we remember to pray for it? Nope. We try to get it ourselves. And we usually mess things up more.''

Then, as was his way, Jim Dillon used his own foibles as a lesson for his congregation. He related how, during his courtship of his wife, he'd had trouble fully trusting God and that by trying to ''help God'' win her back for him, he'd nearly driven her away.

The study went on, but Hope kept going over the beginning in her mind. Was she doing the same thing? Was she refusing to put Jeff in God's hands? She wasn't sure, but she intended to pray for him a lot more and to stop trying to manipulate him. As Pastor Jim had once said, ''We can't drag our loved ones kicking and screaming into the kingdom. They have to choose to walk in hand and hand with the Lord.''

"So, what did you think?'' she asked Jeff at the end of the sermon.

Jeff shrugged. "The guy can sure make an hour fly by. I remember being bored to death in church. At least he's entertaining, and it has to be the first time I've ever seen a preacher in denim.''

Hope's heart fell in spite of Jeff's lighthearted comments. Were the jokes and levity all he'd heard? "Yeah,'' she said, her heart saddened. "He's a nice guy. Listen, I have an appointment to talk with him for a few minutes. Would you mind waiting here while Curt and the band practice and I have my meeting?''

"Sure. It's not like I have a whole lot to do with my time these days. If you and Curt don't have plans for me, I'm pretty unoccupied.''

Hope felt like crying. Was she that demanding? That controlling? She smiled, put her hand on Jeff's shoulder and gave it a reassuring squeeze. "That'll change, I promise. Well, thanks for your patience.'' She backed away. "I shouldn't be too long.''

Jeff watched Hope leave, wondering at her sadness. He'd been serious. It really hadn't been too bad. He looked at the rafters over his head, recognizing aged timber framing. No wonder Dillon hadn't wanted to tear it down. Glancing around, Jeff felt the peace Hope had mentioned. At first he'd thought using a barn for a church was incongruous, at best. Crazed, at worst. But it worked. There was an earthy grass-roots feel to the place he'd never felt in the marble and gilt-edged church his parents had attended on holidays.

"That is one cool chair," a young voice said, calling Jeff back to the present. He stiffened. He'd known it was too good to be true.

"You think so?" he replied tightly, taking in the auburn-haired teen lounging in a chair across the aisle from him.

"Oh, yeah. Mine was clunky and had a mean rattle in the wheels. It was impossible to sneak out of the ward to the toy room without getting caught. Sometimes I think they loosened a bolt or two just so they could keep track of me."

"You were in a wheelchair?" Jeff asked, incredulous, the tension flowing out of him.

The young redhead nodded. "When I was a kid my parents were killed in an car accident. It left me so I couldn't walk. I hurt my back in the crash and had to spend a lot of time at Shriner's Hospital. But the doctors said I had a good chance to walk again and they were right. Is there any chance for you?"

Was there? Jeff wondered. It was hard to remember exactly what had been said before his release, but Curt and Hope seemed to think so. He watched Curt. The therapist was going over chords with the others in the band. He didn't seem the type to pass out false hope.

"There's supposed to be," he answered the boy.

"I'm in therapy working on it. Curt up there in the band on bass is my therapist."

"Boy, are you lucky. My therapist was a lady. She was nice, but I'd rather have had a guy. You know?"

Jeff, noticing a blush heating the kid's cheeks, nodded his agreement. Just then a high-pitched squeal rent the air, and the thunder of small feet resounded in the sanctuary. A tiny-curly haired dynamo barreled toward them. "Mic. Mic," she called, her chubby little arms held out to the teen. She ran full tilt into the boy, whom Jeff assumed must be the sought after Mic.

The teen rolled his eyes. "I'd better find our parents. She has a way of giving Dad the slip. He'll be frantic. You'd think he'd be better at this after our four-year-old sister's terrible twos."

Jeff watched as boy and toddler left the sanctuary and smiled. Would he walk that aimlessly—that unthinkingly—again? If he did, he wouldn't take a single step for granted.

"I see you encountered part of the Osborne clan anyway," Jim Dillon said with a chuckle as he sat where young Mic had been. "That was the youngest and the oldest. Mickey and Leigh."

"He says he was in a chair, too. And that his parents were killed when he was hurt. How can God do that to a kid?"

A shadow passed over the young pastor's face. "A trucker drove too many hours, fell asleep and hit Mickey's family's van. It was the trucker's choice to disobey the law—not God's. Mike and Sarah left four children. Thank the Lord the other three weren't hurt as bad as Mickey. Mike's brother and his wife have raised the four of them since. The little mop top he just carted out of here is their only biological child.''

"So you don't blame God for the bad stuff in life, but you thank Him for the good. Pardon me, Pastor, but how do you justify that? I've got to tell you, I'm not sure I even believe in God." He shrugged. "But then I'm not sure I don't, either. He seems to be the only theory that makes sense. I mean, the world can't be an accident. It seems too complex for that, but if He exists, how can He be so unfair?''

Jim Dillon didn't seem to have a canned response. He thought for a few minutes, his brow crinkled, before he spoke. "God is all goodness. Therefore, good things must come from Him. Man has been corrupt since Adam and Eve fell from grace, so the bad came from man's sin. God uses our mistakes to teach us, but they are our mistakes.''

"You make it sound so simple. What about an accident like mine? How'd that happen?''

The pastor pursed his lips. "That's hard to say. I know Hope blames herself, yet there's never been a kinder, gentler woman. She wouldn't hurt a fly. She says she must have been distracted and missed what looked like heavy wear. She's deeply burdened by guilt over it. We just had a chat about it, in fact.''

"I can't get her to believe that I don't blame her,''

Jeff said, worried for Hope. She was wasting so much time on him.

"She knows you don't blame her, Jeff, but guilt is difficult to get over."

"What can I do for her? She shouldn't be wasting her time on me like this. I keep trying to get her to give up."

"You could accept her help graciously. Let her work through her guilt. If making restitution is her way to do that, then let her. She needs you right now as much as I think you need her."

"You ready to head home?" Hope called as she walked up the aisle from where the band had begun to pack their instruments. Jeff had been so engrossed in his conversation with Jim Dillon he hadn't seen her enter the sanctuary. That rarely happened to him. He was usually so in tune to her presence. It seemed to light a room for him when she entered.

Jim Dillon stood and reached out to shake hands, startling Jeff out of his thoughts. "I enjoyed our talk, Jeff. Come again. You ask thoughtful questions. It keeps a guy on his toes."

Oddly, Jeff thought he might return. The people of the Tabernacle were warm and friendly, and not once, even when questioned by the Osborne kid, had he felt like a side-show freak. Or that he'd been labeled an infidel even after questioning their pastor's sacred beliefs. It was an odd place, this Tabernacle. "I just may do that," Jeff said, as surprised as Hope obviously was by his answer.

It had been a night of surprises. Jeff had thought
the man would act all puritanical and be horribly
scandalized by his and Hope's living situation, even
though she wasn't staying in the house. But instead,
Hope's pastor thought she should stay at Lavender
Hill and work though her guilt. And even more monumental was the surprising fact that tonight Jeffrey
Carrington had come to the realization that he did
believe there was a God. What His role was in the
universe beyond a detached creator, though, Jeff had
yet to decide. But he'd think about it.

He'd definitely think about it.

Chapter Ten

Hope answered the door to the main house the next afternoon and was surprised to find her father standing there. She had missed him terribly, and instinctively a smile bloomed on her face. It was so good to see him. They might argue, but he'd always been a great presence and strong influence in her life. As he wrapped his solid arms around her in an affectionate hug, she tiptoed to kiss his cheek and remembered what she'd always known—they might not agree on everything, but he loved her.

"Dad! Oh, it's so good to see you. I missed you Sunday when I was over for dinner."

"I was busy," he replied, his tone gruff.

"Cole said." He'd also said that her father was busy filling in for her because he'd yet to even try to replace her. It hurt to know she was needed but that Ross wouldn't take her help. She could help Jeff stay on track and keep Lavender Hill running smoothly and still do the more specialized parts of her job for Laurel Glen if only Ross hadn't fired her. It would have been hard, but she could have done it.

"Do you want to come in? I have time right now, but Jeff's working with his therapist."

Ross scowled. "I didn't come to socialize with Carrington."

"Then you came to see me?" she asked, sorry that Jeff was still a sore spot between them. She'd hoped time and distance would soften his attitude and that he had come to see how Jeff was progressing.

Ross stepped inside. "You're the only thing over here that I care about, Hope," he replied, and followed her into the too-bright parlor of Lavender Hill's main house.

"Kat Carrington could have decorated the Parthenon," he grumbled. "This place always reminded me of a mausoleum."

Hope looked at the white, rough-coat walls and marble columns and floors. She chuckled as she walked down the marble steps into the conversation pit in the center of the room. "She did overdo the marble, didn't she? Jeff calls it early Roman hotel lobby."

"That's one thing we agree on," Ross said.

Hope ignored the gibe and tried for a little more small talk. "This room and the formal dining room are the worst. Jeff can't conveniently use this room anymore, of course, which is one of the few inconveniences of his paralysis that he doesn't mind. He just skirts the upper perimeter on his way to the family wing. It has a lovely Italian country kitchen and breakfast nook plus a wonderfully cozy family room. I can give you the grand tour if you want.''

Her father's left eyebrow arched. Hope nearly smiled seeing the exact expression she'd inherited from her father. It drove Jeff crazy. She braced herself, though, knowing any accord between them was quite possibly at an end.

''You've certainly settled in here. I don't approve of you living in residence with two bachelors.''

Any remaining levity fled, and Hope's heart fell. Agitated, she hooked a stray lock of hair behind her left ear. ''Oh, Dad. I thought you knew me better than that,'' she said sadly. ''I haven't settled in. I'm staying in the homestead house around back. And, believe me, when Emily Roberts isn't acting like our mother, she's a bulldog of a chaperone. She even took over a room near Curt and Jeff when we moved them downstairs into the guest wing.''

Hope didn't add that the older woman had moved mainly in case Jeff woke screaming in pain in the night and Curt didn't hear him. She, at least, trusted Hope's integrity.

On the off chance that if Ross knew her presence was doing some good and Jeff was coming out of his depression, Hope added, ''By the way, I'm not sure you care, but Jeff's doing much better.''

''I care. I care that you're wasting your life on a

worthless, selfish cripple. If he was any kind of man, he'd be able to keep going without you sacrificing your career.''

Angry tears sprung to Hope's eyes. "I had hoped your coming here like this represented a change of heart, but I see you're as closed-minded as always.''

Ross shoved his hands into the back pockets of his jeans. "I am *not* closed-minded! Think about what you're doing. What's that saying? 'How far do you have to open your mind before your brains fall out?' I happen to know what I'm talking about where Carrington is concerned. I watched that kid grow up. He drove Addison crazy with his irresponsibility. That boy's faults were all he could talk about.''

"Jeff is far from irresponsible, Dad. Did it ever occur to you that Addison might have been a lousy father? Or that his opinion was colored by unrealistic expectations? Believe me, they were. He was hypercritical, unbending and controlling. Think about it. As disgusted as you've been with Cole, did you ever talk about him that way to a mere acquaintance?

"And Jeff's mother was so involved in her clubs and charities and tennis games that she scarcely noticed her child past his toddler years. Mrs. Roberts was more Jeff's mother than Katrina Carrington was. Have you ever stopped to think how hard Jeff worked to get where he was? To get on the Olympic team you have to be the best of the best, and his place on the team wasn't even in question when he had the accident.''

"So what? He was just after glory. Glory that costs a fortune and gives no return. He was spending every penny Addison ever made, and probably still is. When it's gone, he's not going to know what hit him. I don't want him to pull you down any more than he already has. Look at you. He's turned you into his personal cheerleader and social secretary."

"Jeff is a good and decent man who had his whole world destroyed in one fell swoop. He was lost for a while, but even then he tried to send me on my way. I didn't budge then and I'm still not going to."

"Then you're a fool."

Hope anchored her hands on her hips, trying not to lose her temper. "No, I'm not. That's not the first time you've said that to me. What I am is his friend. When I'm convinced that he's the best he's going to be mentally as well as physically and I know he can run Lavender Hill, then I'll consider leaving, but not before. I think you'd understand how I feel. You share responsibility for his accident. But instead of feeling guilty for the condition of your tack, all you've done is criticize him. Is that how you justify your guilt?"

Ross Taggert stared at her for a long minute. She could see him trying to get hold of his rather formidable temper. "Get this straight, Hope," he said, his teeth gritted. "I am not responsible, nor are you. A rider of Jeffrey Carrington's caliber should have checked his own girth. Besides which, the last time I used that saddle the girth was in perfect condition."

"So it just magically wore out in one ride? Come on, Dad."

Her father turned away, anchoring his fisted hands on his lean hips, then he dropped them to his sides and pivoted to face her. "I came by to tell you that your job is waiting."

"Then I'll be back to work in the morning."

Ross shook his head. "No. I won't condone you living here at his beck and call, but I won't destroy your career the way Carrington is willing to do, either. Officially, you're on a leave of absence. When he shows his true, spoiled colors, you'll be welcome home. We miss you. I'll see myself out."

Hope watched her father's stiff back as he moved into the hall that led to the foyer. The faint squeak of Jeff's wheelchair on the marble tiles alerted her to his presence. She wondered how much he'd heard. She didn't have to wait long.

"So I guess I can lay your father's animosity toward me partially at Addison's feet. I always wondered why Ross had developed such a bad opinion of me."

"His opinion is wrong. He doesn't know you at all."

"But his heart *is* in the right place. He loves you, Hope. Don't throw away something I've always wanted. He's just looking after you. Maybe you should do what he says."

"Are you trying to throw me out again?"

Jeff shook his head and stared at her for a long,

charged moment. Was that longing she saw in his eyes? And if it was, longing for what?

"I should toss you out," he said at last, his voice an octave deeper and a bit strained. "If I was half the man your father is, I would, but I don't want you to leave till you know it's time for you to go."

Hope was startled. What did that mean? That he wanted her there? She had no idea and wasn't sure she wanted to know, so she decided to ignore the comment.

"Well, it isn't time," she replied. "You promised me help on the investment stuff and to tell me what in the world a pick is."

"A pick?" Jeff's forehead crinkled, confusion clouding his expression, then light seemed to dawn in his eyes. He laughed. "Hope, that's a put."

She grinned. "Well, whatever you financial moguls call it. See? Who else is going to teach a lunkhead like me about the stock market if you won't? And you have to tell me what to do with that bill that came for a bunch of AFG stock you bought back in the beginning of February."

"Nothing. I had money in my brokerage account already. It was probably just a notice of withdrawal from the account."

"A brokerage account is different from a bank account? How much time do you have to teach me?" she asked, even more unsure of herself.

"My Viking taskmaster Curt the slave driver had to fix a piece of equipment, so I guess I'm free till he rounds me up." Jeff grew serious again. "I'm sorry, Hope. I hate that I've come between you and your father."

"*You* haven't. *He* has."

Jeff pursed his lips and nodded. "Yeah. Sure," he said, but his disgusted tone made it clear he didn't agree.

"Let's get at that investment lesson," she said, swiftly changing the subject. And wasn't it a shame, she thought as she followed Jeff to the study, that she was more comfortable discussing investments than she was her current relationship with her own father? She had to find a way to show Ross how wrong Jeff's father had been about his wonderful son.

Jeff stared in dismay at the big ebony desk a few minutes later when he moved next to Hope after she settled in the leather desk chair. He'd had no idea he'd left so many things undone since the accident. Shame washed away any feelings her nearness churned up in him. Then, as Hope quickly ran through a summary of all the business she had handled for him, the magnitude of his negligence hit him.

What had he been thinking? Mrs. R and all the other people who worked at Lavender Hill deserved to be paid for their services. Plus there were the suppliers who had gone unpaid, as well. This was a terrible burden to foist on Hope. Her father had been right about him. He'd been incredibly selfish.

He glanced at her serious face as she finished telling him about the household account. Selfish though it might be, he couldn't help being incredibly grateful that Hope had strong-armed her way into his world. She had dragged him, albeit kicking and screaming, from a pit of despair and kept his whole world from caving in around him. He looked away, tempted to take her in his arms and show her all he felt for her. But that would blow his brotherly cover and increase the daily torture of her nearness.

It was then that, in a pile of new mail, he spied the return address of the neurologist who'd handled his case. His thoughts did an abrupt one-eighty. He reached for the envelope at the same time Hope did.

"It's probably another misdirected bill. The right hand sure doesn't tell the left who to bill around that hospital," she quipped, and tore into the envelope, then pulled out a sheet of paper. "Oh, it's a letter from Dr. Chin."

"Here, I'll take care of it," Jeff said quickly. But not quickly enough. He winced when he saw the storm gathering in Hope's eyes. Uh-oh. Busted.

"You missed your checkup right before I came here to stay and you refused the call when they phoned to make a new appointment. Jeff, why?"

"It's too much trouble to go there and sit for hours just to find out nothing's changed."

"What about since then? You're stronger. Maybe the doctor will give us a better idea of what we can expect of your recovery."

Jeff heard the unconscious way Hope made them a

team—a couple. It buoyed his heart for all of two seconds before reality set in. They weren't a team or a couple and wouldn't be, either, unless he managed to stand on his own two feet again. He had to stop kidding himself about his chances, and so did she.

"I still don't want to go. I'm an adult, Hope, and I can decide to see my doctor or not. I decided not to. Simple."

Hope continued to glare. "I'll agree with that. It is simple. And stupid. Why doesn't Curt know about this? I would have thought he'd need to be in touch with your doctor."

Annoyingly, he felt his face heat. "Curt knows. I told him I'd stop cooperating if he blew the whistle. I think he's been talking to the doctor, though."

Hope stared at him for a long moment before asking, "I still don't understand why you refuse to go."

Jeff fisted his hand. "Why? Because I don't want to go," he said, and hated the petulant sound of his voice. Well, too bad! He couldn't go. He just wasn't ready to hear that he'd never walk again. That any idea of a future with Hope was over. He knew it in his heart, but to hear it? No. Not yet. He wasn't prepared to hear the words. He might never be ready. At least now he had hope, and after that talk with the kid at her church his outlook seemed a little brighter. He couldn't give that up. Ridiculously optimistic or not, that was it.

"Of course you're going," Hope said and picked up the phone, evading his attempt to grab it before

she could. "Honestly, you can be such an idiot sometimes," she snapped, then her voice turned pleasant
and impersonal. "Hi, there. I'd like to make an appointment for Jeffrey Carrington. When? As soon as
possible." She glared at him again, her blue eyes dark
and stormy. "Not until then? Okay. It'll have to do.
Thank you. He'll be there."

"You aren't my mother," he shouted when she put
down the phone.

Hope jerked to her feet, looking more upset than
angry. "No. I'm not your mother. I, at least, *care*
about you. I want you to have the future you deserve,
not the one I choose for you. I'd never care what
school you went to or what profession you picked.
I'll still care about you if you never walk or ride
again. The you inside of you is all I've ever cared
about. Do you get the difference between me and Kat
Carrington?"

Jeff watched Hope across the cozy room working
the remote control for the VCR. She had been distant
since storming out of the office on Thursday afternoon. It was Saturday night and Mrs. Roberts, seemingly oblivious to the tension between them, had
rented a new musical comedy that just came out on
video. It was a remake of a 1940s classic. She'd insisted they settle in the family room after dinner, and
they'd just finished watching the old classic version.

"Dear, before you start the new one," Emily said
to Hope, "I think I'll go out to the kitchen and pop

us some popcorn. What's a new movie without popcorn and a soda?"

"Want any help?" Jeff asked, grinning.

Mrs. R glared and huffed out of the room.

Jeff chuckled. She wasn't too happy with him after he messed up her clean kitchen floor. He'd been clowning around, trying to prove he didn't need anyone to teach him how to handle himself in the kitchen. The guy in the video Curt had shown him had made it look so easy. As with everything else in his life since the accident, it wasn't as easy as it looked. In fact, it was really hard. Which is why he'd dropped a jar of spaghetti sauce while trying to get it from the cabinet with the aid of a hand-controlled claw on the end of an extension pole.

He'd thought of having a small handicap-equipped kitchen put in the guest wing near the exercise room. Would it mean he was spoiled if he spent the money to put in a kitchen just for himself? He couldn't forget all the things Ross Taggert had said about him. Selfish. Worthless. Cripple. Did those descriptions fit?

Cripple certainly did, though it was a vicious word. Paraplegic sounded so much less cruel. But a rose by any other name…

He wanted to talk to Hope about his feelings. But if she found out how much he'd heard, it would only make matters that much more strained between her and Ross. It would be the same thing with Cole. With Cole the explosion would be worse. It wasn't Ross's fault, anyway. Jeff's father had poisoned the well years ago, and it had to have been out of jealousy. Jeff would keep his own counsel with both Hope and Cole, but that left him with no one to talk to.

"Would you come to church with us tomorrow?" Hope asked, taking him completely by surprise. They might very well be the first voluntary words she'd spoken to him in days.

Jeff snapped out of his musings. If he agreed, he might get a chance to talk to Hope's pastor. He needed what she called a reality check and he couldn't think of anyone better to turn to than the honest man he'd met Wednesday night.

It was certainly odd that Hope would ask him to go with her just as he'd been wishing for someone impartial to talk with, especially the way things had been between them. He had to fight a grin. He knew how Hope thought. She'd say God was working in his life if he told her what had already been on his mind.

"Okay," he said cautiously, keeping any enthusiasm out of his tone. He didn't want Hope thinking he was suddenly going to go wheeling forward for some sort of altar call or something. "These four walls get pretty boring," he added. "At least it'll be a change of scenery."

Hope nodded, her expression neutral. "That's what I thought, too. Since Curt is scheduled to play at the eleven o'clock service, I thought we'd all go then."

"I'll be ready at what? Ten-thirty?"

"Sharp," she said as Mrs. R came in with a big ceramic bowl of popcorn and a smaller one.

His housekeeper handed the small one to him. It was golden and buttery. Just the way he liked it.

"All for me?" he asked and sent her a grateful smile.

Mrs. R smiled back and tousled his hair the way she used to when he was a kid. It gave him a warm, loved feeling. He guessed he was at least forgiven for the mess he'd made. Whether Hope had forgiven him for manipulating Curt was another thing altogether. Sometimes Emily Roberts made him forget he paid her to take care of him. Sometimes she made him wish she was there just because she wanted to be. He wished the same of Hope. But Emily was there to earn a living, and Hope was only trying to work through her guilt.

Chapter Eleven

Hope watched Jeff and Pastor Jim where they sat toward the back of the sanctuary. They'd been talking only a few minutes when the pastor stood and moved away. Hope's heart fell. She'd prayed constantly since realizing that she'd been trying to help Jeff without divine assistance. But even now, after all that prayer, Jeff had listened once again to one of Jim Dillon's moving messages and hadn't accepted the Lord. She didn't understand how anyone could miss seeing God's perfect salvation as the gift it was, especially when Pastor Jim presented it the way he did. She shook her head. She'd just have to pray longer and harder.

Rome wasn't built in a day. Be patient. He's not ready yet.

He'd apologized for deceiving her and taking advantage of Curt's desire to help him. That had been a major breakthrough for someone raised to believe that he was perfectly within his rights to do whatever he needed to do to get his own way. But there was a new reserve between them that she hoped and prayed would fade.

"So, having a nice time visiting your friends?" Jeff asked as she approached him. The royal blue shirt brought out the healthy glow his skin had taken on in the last few weeks, and his eyes were a clear, sparkling silver today. He might not be ready to accept the Lord, but in his own careful way, he was seeking Him, Hope felt. There was no question that besides the obvious improvement in his general health, Jeff was mentally and emotionally better.

But what were his feelings toward her? He clearly didn't hate her. He'd said he liked her. But did he love her? Only Jeff knew, and he wasn't talking.

She took a deep breath before speaking, tired of weighing every word but afraid not to. "I ran into the pastor's wife. She's such a sweetheart and so excited about the new baby."

"Jim's excited, too. I gather he wasn't around when his son was born. But I got the sense that he's worried about money, too. I had an idea we both may benefit from, so I asked him to stop by Lavender Hill. After the disaster I made of Mrs. R's kitchen, I started thinking about adding a little handicap-equipped kitchenette in the corner of the exercise room. That way if Mrs. R ever has to be gone or is ill, I can handle meals. I remembered you saying Jim did a lot of the work around here, and Curt said Jim used to earn extra money by doing renovation projects on the

side. I figured a chance to earn some extra cash might
ease his mind.''

"Oh. That's such a good idea and it was thoughtful
of you to think of it. I can tell you he does beautiful
finish work. He made that cross up on the altar out
of two old, discarded beams.''

Eyes fixed on the cross, Jeff rolled forward to get
a closer look. Hope blinked her suddenly moist eyes
and prayed that one day she would see him standing
up there looking with love rather than curiosity at the
cross.

Jeff pivoted and sent her a rueful smile, making
Hope's heart do a quick flip. "I think I just hired the
right guy," he told her. "Think he could do anything
with my early Roman hotel lobby?''

Hope laughed. "I don't know. You don't happen
to have a jackhammer in the toolshed, do you?''

Later that afternoon, Hope finished cleaning the
bathroom and was about to start dusting the antique
Shaker furniture in the bedroom when the pounding
of hoofbeats vibrated through the little homestead
house that was beginning to feel like home to her.
She loved the old wainscoting that covered most of
the walls and the high-beamed ceilings overhead.

After setting her dust cloth on the high stone
hearth, Hope went to look out the window. She was
just in time to see Cole dismount from the back of a
horse she'd never seen before. She chuckled. Leave
it to Cole to color-coordinate his mount. The horse's
gleaming coat was the exact same shade of sable

brown as her brother's hair. The mane and tail of his new horse, however, were an astonishing shade of golden-white.

Hope pushed away from the window and zipped through the little cottage to greet her brother.

"And who is this fine young man?" she asked Cole after a hug and peck on the cheek. Automatically she checked the gelding's lines and took hold of the throat latch of his halter. She stroked the white blaze on his forehead, and in the way her father had taught her years ago, she blew a greeting into the horse's nostrils. The big gelding whinnied then butted his head into her chest, knocking her back a step. Hope laughed.

"Don't encourage him. He's bad," Cole growled. "His name is Mischief, and I can't think of a more apt label. It should have warned me, but he was on his best behavior. Till I got him settled in. Or tried to."

"Which is what brings you to my door."

"Guilty."

"So what pushed you over the edge?"

"He pushed Elizabeth into a mud puddle." He scowled at the horse. "And I'm here to tell you it was deliberate."

"Then maybe he's just a smart horse," she quipped.

Cole didn't laugh. He glared. "Not funny, Hope. Your claws are showing. She assures me Jeff is the big brother she never had."

Oh, dear. Not only was she suddenly aware that

she was terribly jealous of Elizabeth Boyer, but it also looked as if Cole was getting serious about her. Hope really didn't want to think about having Reginald Boyer as part of her brother's family. The two would mix like oil and water. And after what Reginald had tried to do to Jeff, she wasn't sure she'd ever be able to be civil to the man. "Sorry. I'm still royally ticked at her father."

"Elizabeth isn't too happy with him right now. That's why she hasn't been by to see Jeff. She's embarrassed by what her father did and isn't too sure about her welcome."

With great effort Hope did the right thing. "It was her father not her who nearly pushed Jeff's head under for the third time," she assured her brother. "Jeff wouldn't hold a grudge. His own father wasn't exactly Mr. Congeniality."

She turned to the horse. "So what other habits do we have to break this bad boy of besides knocking your latest fling into a mud puddle?"

Cole rolled his eyes. "We're just friends, little sister. And as for Laurel Glen's delinquent here," he said, his voice full of affection for his bad-boy mount, "want a list?"

Hope listened to a variety of complaints, all of which she thought were symptomatic of the fear, loneliness and boredom his early life had wrought. Her kindhearted brother had apparently been part of a rescue of the beautiful gelding and taken him on, faults and all.

"Why don't I get this big guy settled as best I can

and we'll see what we can do with him in the next few weeks.''

Jeff heard someone walk into the exercise room but he was bench pressing two hundred and fifty pounds of iron at that moment and didn't dare let himself lose concentration. Curt helped him guide the bar into its rest above the weight bench.

"First class, Jeff," Curt said. "Let's take a break. I'll go get us something to drink. Can I get you something?" he asked Cole who stood framed in the doorway behind Jeff. Jeff gave his friend a wave in the mirror.

Cole shook his head. "That's okay. I just had a glass of tea with Mrs. R."

After a deep breath, Jeff tensed his stomach muscles and curled forward, sitting up without the aid of the bar that hung overhead. It was a new ability he'd mastered only that morning. He didn't use a typical weight bench, of course, but one designed for someone with no power in their legs. But still, Curt said the ability to do a sit-up even on the specialized bench proved that his thigh and calf muscles were strengthening and that his gluteus muscles were responding to his brain's commands again. Jeff hoped so because the doctor's appointment he was dreading loomed ahead. And he really needed good news.

Cole smiled, clearly surprised by the sit-up. "Looking good, dude."

Jeff nodded. "Yeah. I'm doing better. What brings the busy new vet by?"

Cole hopped up to sit on the massage table in the middle of the room. "I shouldn't need a reason, but as it stands I had one. I bought a horse. Rescued, really. He's a beauty. Arabian mixed with who knows what. His past owner's too busy defending himself against animal cruelty charges to be too forthcoming with lineage information. Mischief was up to his haunches in manure when the humane society found him in his stall. He has a few bad habits. Not letting himself be stabled is just one of them."

He related the story of Elizabeth and the mud puddle and was clearly fighting laughter by the time he finished. Jeff had given up the fight long ago and wiped his eyes of gleeful tears. Just thinking of the elegant Elizabeth Boyer dripping with mud, trying to look as stately as she'd been taught to, all the while apparently defending her attacker, gave him the best laugh he'd had in months.

Jeff forced himself to stop howling when Cole started looking a little perturbed. "Come on. Admit it had to be funny. If the queen of England had been dunked in mud it couldn't be funnier. If this hadn't pushed you over the edge, who knows how long you would have gone on getting your rear end nipped and chasing him. So now you brought him to Hope, who's the best person in the county to work with him."

"So Donovan says. He tells me my little sister has a knack with hard cases. Seeing the improvement in you, I'd say it's true."

Jeff grinned. His Hope was one terrific lady. No

wonder he loved her with all his heart, even though he didn't dare admit it aloud.

"You and my sister getting serious?" Cole asked, eyes narrowed.

But it didn't come across exactly as a question, and Jeff was taken aback by the warning tone in Cole's voice as much as the accuracy of the question. "What makes you say that?" Jeff asked, frantically trying to remember what he'd said that would have tipped Cole off to his secret feelings.

"Because your smile just went all gaga at the mere mention of her name."

Jeff frowned. "Don't be stupid. Hope's my friend."

"She'd better be if your face lights up like that when she's not even around. Serious relationships based on less are doomed. I should know. I'm the king of accidentally breaking women's hearts. I don't want to scc hcr hurt that way."

Jeff realized it would be stupid to lie. He'd clearly been found out. When they were kids, Cole had always seen through him any time he'd tried to disguise his feelings. As he'd said to Hope recently, some things never changed. "Okay. I love her. But she hasn't got a clue and she won't if I have anything to say about it."

"If you get that stupid look on your face when she's around, she knows."

Jeff shook his head, his thoughts in panic mode. "She doesn't know and she can't. I can't *let* her know. If she figures out how I feel, she'll never give up on me. She'll never be free. She needs a whole man, and I'm still not sure how much better I'll get. I won't tie her to a cripple.''

"Don't call yourself that!'' Cole snapped, fire in his eyes.

"Why not? Your father does.'' Jeff barked right back then winced. He couldn't believe he'd let that slip. And to Cole, of all people.

Cole jumped from the table. "When did he say that to you?'' he demanded. The fury on his face wasn't a pretty sight, even if it did mean their friendship was still intact.

Jeff raked a hand through his sweat-dampened hair. "When he came by last Thursday. And he said it *about* me, not *to* me. He was arguing with Hope. Please, whatever you do, don't say anything to either your father or Hope. I don't want him hating me more than he already does just in case there does turn out to be a future for Hope and me. And if Hope finds out that I heard Ross, it'll just make matters worse between them.''

Cole subsided and leaned against the massage table. "All right. It stays here between us.''

"Good. But if it's going to stay our secret then you'd better try schooling your own features. You look mad enough to chew steel, and somebody's coming down the hall. It could be Hope.''

"Is this Carrington's health spa? I have an order here for a new kitchen,'' Jim Dillon called.

Dillon didn't look much different than he had when they first met. His jeans were a little more worn and his T-shirt wore the slogan Ask For Directions under the picture of a Bible, but the package was the same. He was a preacher who looked like he belonged in a barn. But then again, Jim's church *was* a barn.

"Jim, come in," Jeff said and reached out to shake his hand. "This is the place, all right. I didn't think you'd get here this fast."

"Are you kidding? And pass up an opportunity like this? Not on your life."

Pastor Dillon looked toward Cole expectantly.

"Haven't you two met?" Jeff asked. "Cole, this is Jim Dillon. Jim, this is Cole, Hope's older brother and my best friend back when we were kids."

Both men shook hands and exchanged polite greetings.

"So do you own your own construction company or just do this on the side?" Cole asked after they'd talked a while about the idea of putting handicap-equipped kitchen facilities in one corner of the exercise room.

"Oh, it's definitely on the side," Jim Dillon answered with a chuckle in his voice.

"Jim's the pastor of Hope's church," Jeff explained when Cole looked confused.

"Oh," Cole said stiffly. His face could have turned to stone for all the animation it had suddenly. He stood. "Well, you two have a lot of planning to do, and I'd better go check on Hope. I imagine she's having trouble with Mischief. Nice to meet you, Pastor. See ya, Jeff. Keep up the good work. And don't try to decide Hope's future for her. She's a big girl. It's her decision who she loves. Not yours." With that Cole fled. Jeff watched him in stupefied silence, wondering if Jim noticed Cole's odd behavior.

"Is it my breath or do I need a shower?" Jim Dillon asked with a crooked grin.

Jeff chuckled. "I'd say it was more your profession. Cole has a real mad on about God. He has since his mother was killed. He blames Him and his father for her death, but I really think he blames himself more."

"Ah. The prodigal son. I'd forgotten about him. Meg's been praying for him for years. I'm sorry if my arrival chased him off. Do you still need to talk or was Cole's parting advice enough help? It sounded right on the mark to me."

Jeff raked his hair off his forehead again. "I can't take his advice. It's more than my not wanting to burden Hope with half a man."

"What exactly is the extent of your injury? Are you saying you couldn't be a real husband to her?"

Jeff thought of the effect her nearness had on him. "No. That's not the problem. I just can't continue to be a burden on her. I may never be whole. Never be someone she can lean on."

"People have all different strengths and we all need different things from others."

"There are other problems. Her father, to be exact. The man can't stand the sight of me."

Jim frowned. "Is it your disability or her living on your estate that's causing the problem?"

Jeff sighed. "Neither, really. In defense of the man,

he didn't want me near Hope before I got hurt. I don't even know if the chair has made it worse or not. He was here on Thursday. I heard the doorbell and by the time I got to the living room they were deep in conversation. At first I didn't want to intrude. Then, before I knew it, I was the subject of heated words between them. The wheels sometimes squeak on the marble so I was trapped in the hall, listening.''

Jim shook his head, a rueful expression on his face. "They say you never overhear good about yourself."

"True. He called me selfish and worthless. Selfish I'll own up to, or Hope wouldn't still be here."

"We talked about Hope's guilt and her need to work through it being one of her reasons for wanting to be here helping you, Jeff."

Jeff didn't know whether he wanted that to be the only reason she was there so she wouldn't be hurt if a deeper relationship between them became impossible, or if he wanted her to love him too much to leave.

"Jim, what you may not realize is how much I needed her when she came here. I'm not going to kid you. I was seriously contemplating suicide. That's when Hope forced her way in here and saved my life."

He couldn't fight the sudden helpless grin memories of her throwing his things out his window brought to his face. "I think she was determined to either shape me up or kill me."

Jim looked around at the exercise equipment. "Well, you aren't dead yet, and she seems to have inspired you to take on life again."

Jeff stared at the floor, and his seesaw emotions plummeted. "But am I still worthless? For a lot of my life my father told me exactly that. Hope's tried to disabuse me of the notion but it's always in the back of my mind. What good am I like this?"

"God doesn't make junk, Jeff."

"So Hope claims."

"Well, here's another truism. People don't get tossed on the scrap heap when they get broken. If Hope's father wants to relegate you to one, you can't let him. You have a lot of things to offer. There are things you can't do. Sure. But there are just as many things you could share with Hope. You can probably even ride again with a special saddle and a horse trained to obey a different set of commands if those are necessary. Besides which, Curt says you're getting better. Who's to say you won't be running rings around her father in a year?"

"He'd still hate me," Jeff replied.

"Let me ask you something. Were you going to let his feelings stop you before the accident?"

Jeff thought back to the night of the Valentine's Day dance and Cole standing behind him on the edge of the dance floor urging him to make up his mind whether he was going to let Ross stop him or not.

"No, I wasn't. But I had more things in the plus column then. Here's a question for *you*. The night I realized I had feelings for Hope, did God know this would happen to me?"

Jim didn't blink. "The Bible says He did. I don't know why He chose not to stop it but I'm sure He could have. That's something between you and Him. And quite frankly that's the only thing I see standing between you and Hope. It's not the weakness of your legs that'll make you less than Hope needs, but the weakness of your faith—of your spirit. That's the strength she'll need you to have. You fell apart when this happened to you. And that's because you had nothing to grab hold of when your body failed you.''

''It was better when I wasn't sure He even existed. Hope says God never fails us, but it feels like He failed me.''

Jim pursed his lips and nodded. ''Right now I bet it does. I can *tell* you He didn't. But that's something you need to believe for yourself. That He didn't is something He has to *show* you. And He will if you give Him a chance. Think about it.''

Jeff promised himself he would think about it later, and they got on the subject of the kitchenette. Then he helped Jim measure the area they decided would make a nice-size kitchenette, and they settled on a counter height that would work for someone in a wheelchair. Jim promised to bring drawings back with a variety of wheelchair-accessible configurations within a week. Jeff had only one stipulation. Nothing colored white unless it couldn't be avoided.

After Jim left, Jeff thought about all they had talked about but he couldn't understand what kind of chance God could possibly need from him. If God could create the world, it seemed to Jeff that He could just wave His hand and fix it all. He should be able to perform a miracle and wipe the last two and a half months off the face of time. But then he remembered a conversation he'd had with Hope about blaming God for the world's ills, and that pesky free will thing got in the way of his theory.

Logic told him it was all double-talk, but his heart—his heart told him the answers lay in the pages of the book Jim had silently left behind on the massage table. And that book was a Bible.

Chapter Twelve

Hope heard the wonderful sound of Jeff's laughter mingled with that of several other men a couple of weeks after Cole dropped Mischief off. She followed the sounds of male camaraderie and good humor down the first floor hall to the exercise room and found Jim, Curt and, surprisingly, Cole with Jeff. They were gathered around some drawings and a catalogue.

Jim had done a preliminary set of drawings and had given them to Jeff at church on the Sunday after he'd been over to look at the room. He'd asked Jeff to think about any changes he might want, and they'd worked on them together later in the week. Jim had painted the walls a muted parchment color in preparation for the rest of the work.

"So you can put these components into cabinets and countertops?" Jeff was saying as he examined the catalogue.

"It's a little more expensive, but I think you'll be happier with the versatility. I wish you'd come down to the kitchen place with me in the morning."

"You don't need to be carting me around with you, and you'd have to drive the big clunky van or I would."

Jim shook his head. "Bad attitude. I won't be carting you anywhere. We'll take my wife's car instead of my truck or your van. You can get in and out of your chair easily enough in here. Why can't you get into the front seat of a car as easily? Just roll up next to it and transfer in. I'll stow the chair in the trunk. No problem. I'd really feel better if you came along to order all this."

"I told you to get anything—as long as it isn't white, I don't care."

"You can't tell me that you don't care," Jim said with a sigh of exasperation in his voice. "Emily told me you worked very closely with the decorator on the kitchen and breakfast room and that most of the ideas came from you. Come on, Jeff. Ask anyone. I'm uncomfortable spending other people's money."

Jeff sighed. "All right. I'll come. But don't say I didn't warn you how much of a production this is going to be."

"Don't worry. So what was this question you wanted to ask me? Something about the Gospel of John?"

Hope tiptoed away from the door, not wanting to intrude. She'd seen the Bible Jim had left for Jeff but hadn't been sure he was reading it. Her heart was gladdened that he apparently was. Jeff had been quiet and a bit withdrawn with her since she'd made the appointment for him with his doctor. And it hurt, but knowing he was questioning and studying helped ease the ache in her heart.

Later that night she saw a light gleaming under his door and wondered if he was all right or if he was suffering from cramped muscles again. She was reluctant to disturb Curt. When she peeked, Hope was surprised to find him sitting up, reading. She could tell from across the room that he held a Bible. About to back out rather than intrude or disturb him, Hope gasped when Jeff looked up.

"What brings you out at this hour?" he asked. He was dressed in sweat clothes, and his hair was mussed as if he'd been asleep but had awakened.

Hope shrugged. "I guess the same thing that has you up and reading. I couldn't sleep. I was passing on my way to the kitchen and noticed your light. I thought maybe you were in pain and being too brave again."

"Nope, chicken to the core."

Curious about what he was reading, she nodded toward the book in his lap. "A little light reading?"

Jeff held up a notepad and grinned. "Hardly. I have a million questions for Jim tomorrow."

"What kind of questions?"

Jeff chuckled, sounding a little mysterious. "This and that. Jim says I keep him on his toes. So far he has an answer for everything," he confided then poked the pad with his pen, "but I've got him this time."

Hope quirked her eyebrow. Jim Dillon knew the Bible inside out and backward. "You think so? He's pretty quick," she warned, grinning. "And speaking of quick, I understand he was here today about the kitchen plans. What did you think?"

Jeff chuckled. "I think you should have just come in and seen them when you were lurking in the hall."

"I didn't want to interrupt the male bonding."

He narrowed his eyes. "Hope, are you avoiding me?"

She shrugged and bit her lip, fighting the tears that sprang too readily these days. He'd been so distant, as if he'd thrown up a wall between them. "I thought it was the other way around," she said as she moved to sit in the chair by the bed.

Guilt flickered in his eyes. "I've been doing a lot of thinking. Maybe I'm just preoccupied."

"No. You've been angry about the doctor's appointment I made for the day after tomorrow. I just want what's best for you."

"I know how that feels," he said cryptically and rushed on as if he'd said too much. Unfortunately, Hope had no idea what he meant.

"I'm not angry," he continued. "Dreading bad news but not angry. If I ever was, it was because you held a mirror up to my own monumental cowardice and it wasn't easy to look at. Sorry I shot the messenger."

Hope chuckled. "It's okay. I'll recover. In fact, I

just did." A yawn grabbed hold of her, and she covered her mouth.

"Oh, stop that," he ordered, smothering his own expansive yawn. They looked at each other and laughed.

"I think maybe I can skip the warm milk. How about you?" she asked sleepily and yawned again. "Ready for bed?"

Any sleepiness that had been there vanished from Jeff's gaze in a nanosecond. The look in his eyes turned suddenly hot. He looked away and snapped his Bible shut. "Go to bed, Hope," he ordered, his voice husky and strained.

Hope stood and retreated to the peace of the homestead house. Unfortunately, her tiredness had fled and her heart pounded even as she pondered the full meaning of what she was nearly sure had been desire in Jeff's gaze.

Did he want her or had she just put them in a compromising situation that would have caused him to react to any woman? A long time later she fell into satisfied sleep, thinking that a sister of any kind would never garner that sort of reaction in Jeff. Jeff seemed to forget she had a brother to compare him with. And this was like comparing apples and oranges.

Two days later Hope pulled up in front of the medical building and glanced at Jeff. He was nervous. Silent and nervous. Wondering exactly what had him so unsettled about this trip, she turned off the engine and pivoted in her seat.

"Want to talk about it? Are you nervous about going out? I thought yesterday's trip with Jim went fine."

"It did, and no, I don't want to talk about it. Why bother? It won't change whatever they're about to find."

Hope was sorry she'd had to force him to do this, but she'd had no choice. She loved him. How could she live with herself if she let him destroy his chance for a normal life?

She had been truthful with herself all along. She knew that by stepping in and taking over, there was a huge chance she could destroy any feelings Jeff had begun to have for her. She no longer thought that had happened. Not after the last couple of days.

A jumpy nervous feeling was her constant companion every time she was in his presence. His gaze on her, shining with desire and tenderness, followed her constantly. But she still had to wonder how long he could withstand the anger she had felt radiating from those same stormy gray eyes all too often before they'd spoken in his room.

"I'm still sorry I had to force you into this," she said. "It's been hard prodding you along, Jeff. But there's no choice for me. Could you stand by and let someone you care about hurt themselves?"

Jeff looked annoyed. "Why do you think I—"

"Why do I think you what?" Hope asked when he abruptly cut off his thought.

He sighed and rubbed the back of his neck. "Forget it. Let's just get this over with."

Hope nodded and turned to open her door as Jeff pushed the side door open and set the lift into motion. She got out and busied herself locking the front door while trying to hide a smile. Had he been going to say, "Why do you think I tried to get you to go home?" She didn't know for sure but she prayed that was what he'd been about to blurt out.

Jeff looked around the waiting room. It was decorated with comfortable sofas and chairs and there were paintings on the walls by a local watercolorist. A kid sat across the room, his arm in a cast. He was busy asking his mother if she thought he'd be able to pitch that season. An older woman with a walker sat reading a magazine, and a young guy with his crutches propped against the wall glanced around the room, clearly impatient to be on his way. Once Jeff would have thought all of them unfortunate to have had their lives interrupted by injury, but now he saw how lucky they were.

Hope put her hand on his shoulder as she walked around him on her way to the reception desk. Her touch startled him and dragged him from his musings. He looked into her concerned gaze. It seemed as though whatever he did hurt or worried her. He tried to smile to put her mind at ease.

When she'd come to his room the other night, he'd been surprised that she'd noticed the reserve he'd tried to hold her in ever since Cole noticed the feelings Jeff couldn't hide. But she had noticed, and worse, she'd misinterpreted his actions and clearly had been hurt, thinking he was angry with her. So he'd dropped the wall he'd been trying to build. He couldn't stand to hurt her.

A memory surfaced of her sitting by his bed during the small hours of the night wearing a pair of old worn hospital scrubs, her eyes suddenly wide and alert as she became aware of the way he'd been looking at her. Jeff fought a grin, remembering how she'd scurried away the moment she'd understood what was in his thoughts.

He wondered who she'd been more afraid of—herself or him. It didn't matter. He liked that he could still make her feel the hidden danger of desire and that her attraction to him could worry her, as well.

I have to get better, Father. You have to help me. I don't think I can stand to cut her out of my life and hurt both of us that way. I will if I have to, but seeing her hurt that way will kill me. I love her so much. Please help me walk again so I can be the man she needs.

"Jeff, are you all right?" Hope asked.

His vision cleared, and Hope's beloved features, tight with concern, came into focus. Jeff realized he'd been praying while staring into space. Which had to mean he believed God listened to prayer and that He must touch the lives of those who call on Him. He grinned at Hope, his heart feeling light in his chest. Jim was right. There probably weren't any atheists in foxholes.

"What are you so happy about all of a sudden?" she asked. "I thought this visit had you nervous."

"I just realized that he can't tell me anything worse than what I've believed all along. And he may have some encouraging news for me instead."

The wait seemed like a year but was really only ten minutes. It seemed as if a whole team of doctors and technicians had something they needed from him, then finally, an hour later, he sat in Dr. Chin's office waiting for the verdict. And verdict really wasn't too strong a word, because whatever the doctor said would affect the rest of Jeff's life. He wished Hope were there, but she hadn't wanted to intrude, saying she'd done enough of that already. He no longer felt that way but she did so he didn't push her. He wished he had.

The doctor walked into the bright office and sat behind his chart-strewn desk. After polite greetings he got right down to business. "I was surprised when I saw your name on the patient list today. I thought you'd given up on me."

"No, I'd given up on me," Jeff replied honestly. "I'm not going to kid you, I really need good news."

"Then I hope I can give it. The prognosis is still about the same."

Jeff felt his heart stutter in his chest then fall still. But wait—he'd said he hoped he would be giving good news. That made no sense, and Jeff said so.

Doctor Chin smiled. "I wondered if you'd even heard me when you were in the hospital. Now I know you didn't. I told you improvement could be slow but as long as there was improvement and as long as you don't plateau at any stage for too long, there's every chance for you to regain full use of your legs.''

"It didn't sound like that.''

"No. I don't imagine to a young vital man at the top of his sport that it would have sounded encouraging, but that's what I said and it was meant to be encouraging.''

"I felt as if I wasn't getting better when I was released.''

"That's because nowadays hospitals are to save lives. Often people go home to mend and do it much faster away from the hospital environment. The rehab we recommended would have been such a place. I have to agree that though, when I look at your progress at home with a private therapist, yours was a better course of action. So now for further encouragement. Thus far you haven't stopped progression. The muscles in your legs are strong. The swelling in the spinal cord is slowly reducing. I would have liked it if it had gone down sooner as it does in others, but it was pretty bad and every individual is different. You have much better sensitivity and reflexes in your legs and feet, as well. The gluteus muscles are responding, as Curt Madden mentioned in his report. You just need to keep going with your therapy. Try not to get discouraged. Curt wants to have you fitted for braces to get you up using parallel bars, and now that I've seen your progress, I agree that it's nearly time. Keep your eye on the prize, Jeff, the way you must have with the gold medal, and you'll win this battle.''

Jeff thought of the prize—his prize—and it was nothing so transient as glory and a medal. His prize would be Hope. His shining goal was a love to last a lifetime. But now he had something more solid than his own strength to call on for courage and perseverance. He had a Father to turn to in moments of discouragement. He had a Savior to lean on when failure made him feel worthless. He had the Spirit of God to strengthen him in the coming weeks.

And, he realized with a sudden flash, he had real friends. Hope. Curt. Cole. Jim. And Emily Roberts. He'd always had Mrs. R, who loved him with a mother's love, even if she did draw a salary. For weeks she'd stayed without one. He'd discovered that when he'd checked the payroll figures for Hope. Emily had written checks for others on the account in those first weeks after the accident before Hope came, but she'd written none for herself. He was a little ashamed for not seeing her as more than a housekeeper and for keeping her on the outskirts of his life.

Later that night in the quiet of his new room Jeff gave his heart and his life to the God of the Bible that Jim had given him. As peace and love wrapped around him, he realized that, even if he never walked again, the accident was the best thing that ever happened to him. Because, as Jesus said, *For what will it profit a man if he gains the whole world, and loses his own soul?*

He couldn't wait to tell Hope.

Chapter Thirteen

At the end of that Sunday's service, Jim gave his usual altar call, and Hope said a quick prayer that Jeff would one day heed the call of the Lord. As the congregation began singing the final song there was a stirring next to her and the sound of Jeff releasing the brake on his wheelchair. She turned in time to be on the receiving end of one of his heart-stopping grins, then he pushed forward toward the altar. Tears of joy fell unbidden as Hope turned the other way into the arms of her aunt Meg, who was sitting with them. The two women hugged then watched Pastor Jim lead the four who'd gone forward in a prayer while the rest of the congregation continued to sing.

"Why didn't you tell me?" Hope asked Jeff after hugging the daylights out of him a few minutes later.

"I was going to but I decided to make a public profession first. I didn't tell Jim, either. He was as surprised as you probably were." Jeff reached up and dried her tears. "He didn't blubber all over me, though."

"Oh," she said, embarrassed, wiping her tears. "Sorry. I'm just so happy for you."

"I'm pretty happy for me, too." He took her hand and gave it a quick squeeze. "Let's celebrate. Brunch at the Hotel Dupont. What do you say?"

Hope nodded, and they were on their way. Jeff drove, having practiced using the hand controls around the property that week. He started a discussion on current events and, taking her cue from him, she stayed away from personal topics. They teased each other about childhood and adolescent escapades, then moved on to solving the problems of Cole and her father and Aunt Meg. Jeff's solution was to lock her brother and father in a room with Jim Dillon as referee until they kissed and made up. He also wanted to find a nice old guy for Aunt Meg. Hope laughed, saying she liked Pastor Jim too much to make him suffer like that and that Aunt Meg wasn't old at fifty. Jeff conceded the point and revised his prescription to a guy in his prime but said Jim was tougher than he looked.

Laughing and talking, they moved to the entrance of the exclusive restaurant and waited to be seated. After several minutes a man approached from the back of the restaurant.

"Mr. Carrington, how good it is to see you."

Jeff looked up and smiled as if greeting an old friend. "Thanks, Malcolm. It's good to be out and about. How have you been?"

"Fine, Mr. Carrington. Business is as good as ever." The tall thin maître d' looked concerned and pensive for a moment. "I'd heard about your injuries. I hope everything turns out all right."

"So far, so good. Do you have a table available that will help me impress the lady?"

Malcolm laughed. "But of course," he replied in a terrible French accent. "Jez follow moi."

Hope laughed, as well, but she *was* impressed by the beautiful room. The chandeliers glowed, and the tablecloths gleamed a bright snowy white and set off the brilliant colors in the fragrant, fresh flowers that graced the tables.

"So tell me when you made your decision," Hope asked as soon Malcolm had seated her and they were alone. "I know you well enough to know it didn't come suddenly this morning."

"No. There wasn't any blinding moment of total discovery. At first I was just curious about what made a man like Jim Dillon become a pastor. It's clear that he could run his own construction firm and make a mint. I couldn't understand why he'd give up a chance to do something he clearly loves to be a pastor. So I started asking questions to see what it was that attracted both of you to religion. As we talked, though, I came to realize that it wasn't religion but faith in God Himself that was the driving force.

"Then, when I was in the doctor's office, I found myself praying that the news would be good. I had already come to the place where I realized that I did believe in God, but I thought of Him as this great overseer in the sky who sat up there watching us and shaking His head at the messes we made of our lives. If there was any one moment, suddenly finding myself praying was it. Once I faced the fact that He would involve Himself in our lives, it all made sense—His plan for salvation, right down to my accident.''

Hope reached across the space between them and took his hand where it lay on the table. She forced herself to ignore the little frisson touching him always gave her. This was about something more lasting than earthly needs and wants.

"Jeff," she said seriously, "the accident was my fault. Not God's. He doesn't hurt us."

"I know, but Jim says that sometimes God will let us get hurt and use the evil for good. So I got to thinking that this accident may have been the best thing that ever happened to me. I'd never have taken the time to really look at my life and what was missing if I hadn't been forced to. God certainly knew if no one else did how hard you've tried over the past few years to get me to see where I was headed. But I'm not headed there any longer."

Hope smiled, albeit bittersweetly. "I'm glad you're not, but I still feel guilty about causing you to get hurt."

"I don't want you to stay at Lavender Hill because you feel guilty for the accident."

"I stayed because you needed me." *And you don't now.*

"And I did. I can't believe how wrong I was." Jeff

shook his head and grinned sheepishly. "Why you didn't smother me in my sleep, I'll never know. And I'll never be able to repay you for all you've done."

"This wasn't about repayment. It was about..." She hesitated, unable to bring herself to declare her love after he'd claimed she was only a sister to him. She still doubted that he'd meant it, but she had her Taggert pride and she was terribly afraid it was all she would have left after this brunch was over. Jeff didn't need her anymore. He had the Lord to lean on. She really had no more reason to stay.

Unless he gave her one, and she didn't think he'd come that far. To cover what any second would be an uncomfortable pause, Hope coughed then continued. "It was about friendship."

Jeff felt a cold sweat coat his body. Did it sound as if she meant to leave Lavender Hill? That was what he'd been trying to achieve all along, wasn't it? He should be relieved, but instead a cold dread filled him. He didn't need her for emotional support or to kick his rear into gear the way she had. And it wasn't as if he'd never see her again or she wouldn't visit. Hope was too strong to let her father influence her to stay away. So why was he in this sudden panic?

Maybe, he decided, it was the potential of losing the closeness of sharing duties at Lavender Hill. She'd settled into overseeing the breeding operation and the care of the horses, and he'd taken over handling his investments and the bookkeeping during the hours he wasn't working on his therapy.

No. Wonderful as sharing his life and work with her was, it wasn't what he would miss. He would miss seeing her arrive still sleepy-eyed for breakfast. He would miss the intimacy of knowing she was near. It was Hope, the pure, shining essence of the woman he loved, that he would miss for the rest of his life. Hope. Just Hope.

The waiter's arrival at that moment was a welcome distraction. After listening to the day's specials, they ordered. Jeff noticed Hope assessing him with that bright blue gaze of hers. "What?" he asked.

"Why have you resisted going to a full-service farm? With the renewed interest in equestrian competition and just plain weekend pleasure riding, why did you decide to limit yourself to breeding and sales with all those stalls just sitting vacant?"

"Because I had a dream. I wanted to start a top-quality Olympic training facility. But I wanted to be able to offer scholarships. That's where the breeding came in. That was supposed to provide for the scholarships and the seed money to get the facility started without filling the stables with other people's mounts and my taking the time to hire a lot of people I'd just have to supervise."

Hope frowned, confusion clouding her gaze. "Where'd this idea for a training facility come from?"

Jeff understood her surprise. He hadn't shared his idea with anyone. Not even Hope. She'd thought he was aimless, but he hadn't been. Not totally. He'd just been rudderless, running through life without

God's grace to show him the way. Now he wanted to share it with her, the way he wanted to share everything in his life with her.

"The idea's been kicking around in my head for a while," he said. "It started a few years back with a girl several years younger than me whom I'd seen in local competitions. She was the most naturally talented rider I've ever seen and she was moving up quickly in the rankings. She had incredible presence on horseback. You just knew that animal would do anything she asked of it. She had such potential. Then she vanished from the scene. I later learned that her parents had been killed. She and Grandfather couldn't keep up with the family's horse farm and certainly not the expense of keeping her in competition. They eventually lost everything. It's always bothered me." He shook his head in disgust. "What an incredible waste of talent."

"So poor kids would get scholarships?"

"If they had the talent and drive to make it. And if that drive came from themselves and not pushy parents. Also, the scholarships would include competition expenses."

"So others like the girl you remember wouldn't be lost. It sounds wonderful."

Jeff wanted it so badly he could taste it. It was the same way he wanted her in his life. Neither seemed possible right then. Not if he couldn't get on his feet again.

Unless he had help.

Jeff's heartbeat picked up and doubled its beats. Unless Hope wanted to help...

He knew he should encourage her to go back to her job at Laurel Glen. He almost held his tongue, but then he looked at her animated expression, and his resolve melted. It was a chance to keep her close. It would be torture, but so would not seeing her every day. And now that it was apparent that her time at Lavender Hill was coming to an end he didn't think she looked particularly happy about it. Maybe a partnership was all they'd ever have. Maybe it would be enough for both of them.

Jeff took a deep breath and plunged ahead. "Hope, would you be interested in a partnership? I can't very well teach riding from a chair."

"Work at your training facility?"

"Our facility," he corrected. "I wouldn't be able to do it without you."

A smile bloomed on her face but just as quickly vanished. "But you'd be putting up all the capital."

Jeff pursed his lips, thinking. "What was your father paying you?"

Hope named a figure, and Jeff felt his eyebrows climb his forehead in surprise. Ross really had needed to beg in order to get his daughter back on the payroll. "That much?" He smiled, loving the irony of it. "Well, I hear you're worth it. Suppose you draw twenty-five percent less than that and put that twenty-five percent up against what I put into the project to get us started. Before you know it, you'll be a full partner."

Hope bit her lip, a frown still making a little crease between her eyebrows. "I'm not trying to discourage you, but what if we fall flat on our faces? You're taking all the risk."

"I don't think so. What will your father's reaction be to this?"

"Ever see the footage of Old Faithful going off?" Hope gave him a sardonic grin, but he saw worry in the set of her jaw and in the depth of her blue eyes.

"So you *will* be taking a chance. Ross won't hold your job if you sign on to work on this with me. And I imagine living at home will be more than a little difficult. You're welcome to stay on in the homestead house, of course.

"I had planned to move in there if I ever got this off the ground, but it's impossible with the chair. I won't destroy the historical value of that house with all the alterations I'd need to live there. With God's grace it would be a waste, anyway, because I'll be walking before we're ready for students. If He has a different plan for me, I'll just take over the bottom floor of the guest wing as an apartment. The kitchen's almost done, anyway." He shrugged carelessly but felt anything but careless while considering the possibility that he would never walk again—that Hope would never be more than a friend and a business partner.

She reached out and squeezed his hand again. His heart stuttered then took off like a runaway horse, reminding him how much he wanted this to be so much more than a meal shared by friends and partners.

He looked up from their hands to be snared by her keen sapphire gaze. "You won't be less of a man than you were if you don't walk again. You know that, right?" Hope demanded.

Jeff smiled wryly. Leave it to Hope to key in on his fears and not see the desire he felt for her. "But my life would be limited, Hope. I guess we'll just have to wait and see."

"And pray. Don't forget about that." She put her other hand over the one she already held. "And, Jeff, there's something else you need to pray about."

"The success of the school."

She shook her head, and her gaze snagged his. "You have to pray for the grace to live your life the way God wants you to live it, not the way you think you need to live it.

"The same goes for me," she continued. "I have to do what God wants me to do. I have to live the plan that He wants me to live. To honor Him, I can't do anything that even smacks of immoral behavior. I appreciate the offer of the homestead house, but I can't go on living there, Jeff. I came to get you working toward life again, and you're well on your way. It wouldn't look right if I stay, with you regaining your health."

Jeff stared at her. She was right. The only reason there wasn't talk yet was that most of the community considered him an invalid. Even in this modern age of people living together, sleeping together before marriage, Hope's reputation, unlike his, had always been above reproach. Her air of innocence and the sheer purity of her beauty had drawn him to her in ways none of the sophisticated women he'd been involved with over the years had. He knew that about her, but others didn't, and Jeff didn't want Hope subjected to even a hint of scandal.

"Where has my head been? I'm so sorry. I never even considered that anyone would think— I—I guess you'll be going back to Laurel Glen."

"No. You're right about my father. I refuse to go back home and fight with him every waking moment I'm there. I'd wind up with the sort of relationship with him that Cole has. There have been enough harsh words said between us already. I'll start looking for a place of my own but I'd like to stay on till then."

"You're welcome, of course," he said, but he hated the idea of her finding an apartment or a house. He hated the idea of her losing Laurel Glen. But more, he hated that he'd caused a rift so severe between her and Ross that she felt she had to live elsewhere.

"Maybe you could talk to Ross again," he suggested. "Maybe if he sees that I've got real plans for a future, he'll object less to our partnership. And if you're not living there…"

Hope shrugged. "I'll try, of course, but Dad is nothing if not stubborn."

"Well, you're certainly welcome to the homestead house for as long as you want to use it. I wish you were staying, or at least going back home, but I understand your feelings."

What Jeff didn't understand was what had turned Ross against him. That had been the worst year of his life. First Marley Taggert had been killed and Cole had gone off the deep end. Jeff had tried to keep him from doing anything too crazy, hoping to hold the only real family he'd ever known together.

Next his father had refused to fund his equestrian competitions unless Jeff went to Penn. He'd gone to Ross for advice, as he often did. Ross had said an Ivy League degree certainly wouldn't hurt him, and he'd advised Jeff to buckle down and try to get the grades he'd need to get in to Addison's alma mater. Jeff had, but then it had all fallen apart anyway.

One night during semester break, Cole had come over after an argument with Ross. Jeff had usually been able to calm his younger friend down, but Jeff had an appointment with a tutor that night, and Jeff's mother had insisted Cole leave. Cole had gone looking for trouble and found it in the guise of a police cruiser with its motor running. He'd gone on a joy ride, been caught, arrested and given the dubious choice of military school or juvenile detention with the possibility of being charged as an adult.

Jeff hadn't known why, when he came home that spring, he was no longer welcome at Laurel Glen. Now he knew that once Cole was gone Addison must have started poisoning Ross's mind. Jeff supposed Ross might have thought Jeff had been a bad influence on Cole and therefore was the author of all the family troubles.

Whatever the cause, Ross's cold anger toward Jeff had been uncomfortably evident, so he'd withdrawn from Laurel Glen except for riding occasionally with Hope when they'd meet at the border of the two properties. At least with Hope as his partner, he wouldn't finally lose it all.

Chapter Fourteen

No you don't, Hope thought. You don't have a clue why I'm leaving!

And at that moment she knew beyond a doubt that she'd made the right decision. Perhaps it was only a matter of time until Jeff saw that she didn't find him wanting because his legs no longer worked. Perhaps he'd even walk again. But she also had to accept that his new faith in God didn't guarantee that he'd come to see himself the way she did.

If she had to settle for being his partner, she would. Seeing him every day, working with him, most certainly would be better than only the occasional visit. And she couldn't go on living at Lavender Hill in the hope that he would regain his ability to walk or that he would come to a place about his paralysis where he could truthfully finish the conversation he'd begun on the hilltop just before his accident.

To wait around, living in his pocket while he kept

her at a distance, would have been emotional suicide. He had God in his life now and could lean on Him for strength in difficult times. So it was time for her to leave.

Maybe she could repair her relationship with her father. And maybe—just maybe—if she wasn't quite so convenient to Jeff and if he had the chance to miss her when she was gone, he just might wake up. Maybe then he'd look past his pride and move fully into the future whether he was walking or rolling forward.

Late for dinner, Hope stopped dead in her tracks the second Jeff looked up from his plate. His right eye was on its way to a classic shiner, and his cheekbone wasn't far behind on the color scale. "What on earth happened to you?"

Jeff and Curt exchanged twin guilty looks.

"Did you two have a fight or something like that?"

Jeff was instantly indignant. "Of course not! Do we look that juvenile?"

Hope put a hand on her hip. "Actually you look like a couple seven-year-olds caught with their grimy little hands in the cookie jar. What do you think you look like?"

"I think you're too nosy," Jeff complained. "If you must know, I fell. Okay? Could we drop it at that? It's embarrassing."

Hope nodded, hating that she'd upset him, but then she caught another odd look between the men. What were they up to?

"How goes the apartment hunt?" Emily asked as she set a warmed plate of food at Hope's usual seat.

Hope sat and said a quick silent grace before answering. It was a depressing topic. "It isn't. Two weeks and all I've seen are a ton of uninspiring boxes the builders stacked along hallways and on top of one another. I've come to the conclusion that apartment complexes are just not my cup of tea. Then there were the three cottages she took me to today. They turned out to be nothing more than falling down shacks sitting at the edge of three equally dilapidated farms. Anything else the real estate agent found so far is either way out of my price range or too far from Lavender Hill."

"We could up your salary draw," Jeff suggested. "It would take a little longer for you to be a fully vested partner but—"

"No. I'll find something. You're risking too much on your own with this as it is."

"Are you sure you don't want to go back to Laurel Glen?" Jeff asked.

Hope shook her head. "After Ross's reaction to my decision to work with you on the training facility there's just no way I'm going to move back home and continue to argue with him every time we run into each other. Even short visits are getting more and more strained."

Ruby, her personal horse, felt Hope's restlessness when Hope went over a couple times a week to ride her. She should bring the mare over and stable her at Lavender Hill, but that felt so much like cutting her ties to home that she couldn't bring herself to seriously consider it.

Though she resisted the idea, Hope knew she should do it. The last time she'd seen her father had been anything but pleasant....

"You're actually going to work for him?" Ross had demanded when she'd told him about the training facility. "Hope, this is insane. Jeffrey Carrington opening a school? I know what the equestrian world is like. Between events those people have affairs and change partners the way the rest of us change clothes. Carrington running a training facility is like asking a fox to guard a henhouse."

Hope fisted her hands at her sides. Her father was the only person other than Jeff who could make her this mad. Maybe because she loved them both so much. "That's beyond insulting! Jeff would never take advantage of a young girl. That isn't the kind of person he is. If he was ever as promiscuous as you say, then he's changed. I told you that he'd accepted the Lord and that he's going to church with me now. He's become friends with Pastor Jim. You're wrong and you're too stubborn to give him a chance."

"And you're blind. This whole thing is just too convenient. He decided to open this facility right about the time you say he stopped slipping back into his so-called depressions. Don't you see? He's using this facility to hold on to you."

Hope had smiled. "Forget it, Dad. If that were true,

it would mean that my fondest wish had been granted.''

Emily put a drink to the right of Hope's plate and called her back to the present. ''No, I won't move back there,'' she told Jeff. ''Aunt Meg doesn't need my presence adding more tension to that house.''

Jeff grimaced. ''I'm sorry. I should never have asked you to work on this with me.''

''I'm not a child, and my father has no right to pick my friends.''

''He loves you. It's a gift some of us never got. Don't waste it, Hope.''

She gave an unladylike snort. ''Why tell me? Tell him. He's the one who won't even consider changing his mind.''

Jeff lifted the receiver of the phone then dropped it in its cradle. He sighed. What was that? The tenth time in as many minutes that he'd chickened out on making the call?

This was ridiculous. He'd known Ross Taggert his entire life. Because Addison had gotten rid of all the animals when he'd inherited Lavender Hill, it had been Ross who'd put Jeff on a horse for the first time. It had been Ross he'd run to for advice in the confusing teen years when Jeff had been pulled in so many directions at once by his own needs and wants and those of his father, which had been diametrically opposed to his own. And now the man he'd grown up thinking was the ideal father hated the very sight of him.

But that wasn't Jeff's fault. He'd done nothing to deserve it. Somehow he had to convince Hope's father of that, then reach some kind of accord with him. Jeff couldn't let her lose what he had craved over a lifetime. He couldn't let her be hurt that way and not try to make things better.

Before he could change his mind, Jeff lifted the receiver and dialed Ross's office number.

"This is Ross Taggert. I'm busy on another line. Leave a message and I'll get back to you."

Jeff ground his teeth. He hated answering machines. "Ross, it's Jeff Carrington," he said into the mouthpiece. "It's about Hope. Could you call me right back?"

Ten minutes later Ross Taggert charged into Jeff's office. "Is Hope all right?" he barked, then stopped in his tracks, his gaze riveted on Jeff's bruised face. "Were you two in an accident? Where is she?"

Jeff fought a smile. Yeah, Ross was a real tough guy. His voice was shaking as much as his hands. Jeff wondered what it must be like to have a parent care about you like that.

"Relax. Hope's just fine," he told her father. "She isn't even here. I'm sorry I worried you. The bruises have nothing to do with Hope except that I got them in therapy and she's the one who got all that started."

Ross heaved a deep sigh and sank into the green leather wing chair opposite Jeff. He raked a trembling hand through his hair then braced his elbows tiredly on his thighs. His shoulders sagged as he let out another deep breath.

"If she's fine then why the call?" he asked, sitting back in the chair and pinning Jeff with his arresting blue eyes, so much like his daughter's.

"Physically she's fine but she misses her family. Specifically her father, since Cole visits here and she sees Meg at church all the time. I'll get right to the point. We have something in common, you and I. Hope. You love your daughter, and it might surprise you to know that I do, too."

"You don't know the meaning of love." Ross sneered.

"That was once all too true," Jeff conceded, trying to be polite. "Love is something I never had, which is probably why I didn't recognize it until it may have been too late."

"What do you mean, it may have been too late?" Ross asked, his face fixed in a deep frown.

"We have something else in common. You don't want Hope tied to a cripple. Well, neither do I. And if I can't get myself on my feet, she'll never know how I feel."

"You heard my argument with Hope about you," Ross said, looking uncomfortable and embarrassed. "I spoke in anger."

"I am a cripple, though I prefer paraplegic. But I'm not content to stay this way. I'm not giving up. If there's any way I can walk again, I will. Then, and only then, will I tell your daughter how I feel. And

I'll ask her to marry me at the same time. I'd like your blessing.''

''That's not going to happen,'' Ross growled.

''Then you'd be the loser. And Hope would lose, too. I'm sorry, Ross. You also called me selfish that day, and I guess I am. I'm not giving up the only person who's ever loved me because you want to believe things my father said about me. You never really respected his opinion about anything else. I don't know why you chose to about me.''

''Because he was your father. Why would he lie? And how can you say your parents never loved you? They gave you every advantage. You went to the best schools. Had the best of everything.''

''No. I didn't have the best of everything. Maybe from the outside looking in I did, but I didn't. Hope and Cole—*they* had the best. They had parents who loved them for who they were. Kids don't care about money. They care about love. They care about acceptance. They care about respecting their parents. If you couldn't respect Addison, what makes you think I could?''

Ross nodded but he didn't look as if he'd changed his mind about anything. ''Is that all you had to say?'' he asked, the forbidding frown still on his face.

''No. It's not. I never meant to come between you and Hope but I have. I wanted to try to show you that your worries are unfounded. I love her. I promise not to ever intentionally hurt her and I don't want to see her hurt by anything any more than I think you do. But you *are* hurting her. You've all but lost Cole.

Please, Ross, don't make the same mistake with Hope. I wanted you to know how far this has gone with her. She's moving off Lavender Hill, but she won't even consider moving home to Laurel Glen because of the tension between you.''

Ross stood. He looked both thoughtful and confused. "I appreciate your honesty and your concern for Hope. I guess you've given me a lot to think about. As for Hope moving off on her own, it may be for the best. Things aren't very good at Laurel Glen right now.''

"If it's financial—"

"I'll handle it," Ross said, shaking his head. He hesitated, then reached over the desk and offered his hand. "For what it's worth, I'm sorry about the accident. If any of us contributed—"

"Don't." He took Ross Taggert's hand and said a quick prayer as he shook it that this meant a new accord between them. "I should have checked the girth myself, Ross. You were right about that. I've tried to tell Hope from the beginning but she's as stubborn as her father.''

Jeff grinned and added, "And maybe this talk should stay between us. Hope doesn't know how much I heard that day. Better to let sleeping dogs lie.''

Ross nodded. "I'll be in touch," he said with a small smile and left.

Jeff was struck by how young the man looked when he smiled. He couldn't help wondering why so nice-looking a man had remained alone for fourteen years. Jeff imagined Ross Taggert could have had any woman he wanted. Which meant he still wasn't interested. How long could grief last?

Then Jeff thought of the very real possibility of losing Hope, and he realized he had one more thing other than love for Hope in common with Ross. He, too, would love only one woman in his lifetime.

Chapter Fifteen

Hope heard Curt's shout of joy as she came in the
back door for breakfast, then Manny's distinctive accent rang out, though she couldn't understand what
he'd yelled.

"What's going on?" she asked Emily as the housekeeper stomped into the kitchen, an annoyed expression tightening her face. "They're really whooping it
up down there."

"I'm beginning to think they've turned into mad
scientists. Yesterday a parcel arrived addressed to
Jeff, and I took it down to the exercise room. 'What
is it you've ordered now?' I asked, just moderately
curious. 'A secret,' said Jeffrey, and then he snickered, wheeled away and handed the package off to
Curtis. Then Curtis proceeded to open it, but he
stopped when he noticed me still standing there. He
closed the box and pretty as you please said, 'Was
there something you needed, Mrs. Roberts?' Dis-

missed from the room like a gossipy servant. As if I'd pry into my Jeff's private business. I know my place.''

Hope didn't think it was the exact time to point out that she'd referred to Jeff as hers.

Emily anchored her work-worn hands on her ample hips. ''It was just natural curiosity. I've never been a nosy sort. I just wondered if it was some newfangled thing or another for that little kitchen of his. Or if maybe it was something for his therapy. Really, I just can't—''

''Emily! Calm down,'' Hope demanded but took the sting out of the order with a bright smile. Hope had never seen the elderly woman so flustered. ''You're going on at a mile a minute. I'm sure they're not up to anything nefarious. This is Curt and Jeff we're talking about.''

''But the door was locked just now. And Manny is in there.''

''They wouldn't open it to you? Maybe Jeff wasn't dressed.''

Hope had to fight a grin when Emily's lower lip pouted and she slammed a pot onto the stove top. ''They told me to go away! Well, let me tell you, if I'm not wanted, then far be it from me to insinuate myself. I should let them cook their own breakfasts. That's what I should do.''

''Well, now *I'm* curious,'' Hope said. ''And I *will* insinuate myself. I going to investigate. I'll warn them their future meals are in jeopardy. That ought to straighten them out.''

Hope left Emily still banging pots and headed for the exercise room. Expecting to find it locked, she was surprised when the knob turned smoothly under her hand.

"Hello, the laboratory," she called, pushing open the door. Curt and Jeff were seated at a table working on a three-dimensional puzzle of a medieval castle that Curt had started several nights before. An odd activity for the time before breakfast when they usually worked on a little therapy.

"Since when is this a laboratory?" Jeff asked, confused.

"Since you two started being so secretive. Emily thinks you have Frankenstein's monster hiding in the bathroom."

Jeff's gray eyes widened, sparkling with humor. "Secretive? Curt, have we been secretive?" he asked.

"Not that I'm aware of," Curt answered as he fitted another puzzle piece into the developing structure.

There'd been something conspiratorial about the tone of both men's voices. Hope shot them a narrow-eyed glare. "Then why was the door locked?"

Jeff frowned, but there was a teasing lilt to his voice when he asked, "Was the door locked when you came in?"

"No, Jeff, the door was not locked when I came in," Hope answered tightly. She saw why Emily was so upset. They were double-teaming her and they definitely were hiding something. And Hope didn't like it any more than Emily had.

Jeff scratched his head in what Hope felt to be

feigned bewilderment. "Then why'd you say it was locked?"

"You two—no, I heard Manny, so there are three of you—have hurt poor Emily's feelings both yesterday and today. She's ready to go on strike. I want to know what you're up to."

"Should we show her?" Curt asked.

Jeff looked suddenly worried. "Maybe not yet."

"You did it before," Curt argued in answer to some silent communication between them.

"I also fell flat on my face the first time." Jeff looked at her. Hope didn't know what he saw, but he nodded and spun away from the table toward the parallel bars.

"Manny!" he called. "You can come out now. The cat's out of the bag."

The bathroom door opened and a dark head peered around the door. "Cut? Bug?"

"Old expression," Curt told him. "It means the secret's out. Come on. Jeff's about to put on a show for Hope. Just do what you did last time."

Jeff looked at Hope and gave her a nervous smile. "Now don't go getting your hopes up. This isn't as big a deal as it looks. It's mostly arm strength and braces."

For the first time Hope noticed that there were heavy braces strapped over his gray sweatpants.

"But it's the first step onto the next part of the road," Curt said encouragingly as he stood between the bars in front of Jeff. Manny took up a position at the back of the wheelchair.

Jeff was going to try to stand! The moment the saddle separated from Prize's back suddenly flashed across her mind's eye. Once again, as if in slow motion, she watched Jeff impact with the hard winter ground. She saw him grimace in pain. She saw him go slack.

Hope was suddenly horribly nervous. Not because she didn't want Jeff to walk again. Of course that wasn't it. But he was safe in his wheelchair. What if he fell? What if he did more injury to his back?

He'd said he'd already fallen! The bruises made so much sense now. Her stomach dropped, and she watched in silence as Jeff grabbed the bars. Hope instinctively closed her eyes, unable to watch when she saw his muscles bunch with the effort.

Please, Lord, don't let him get hurt.

"Hope, open your eyes before you miss the show," she heard Curt say.

She did as ordered and found herself drawn to Jeff's side, her gaze instantly locked in place by his. "You're standing," she said unnecessarily.

"On my hands," he said a little breathlessly as he looked down at her. "I'm not sure it counts exactly...but it's more than I could do a month ago."

"You're so tall," Hope told him, then felt a little foolish, but it had been so long since she'd looked up into his handsome face. She wanted so badly to touch him that she had to clench her hands behind her back to stop herself.

"Nah. You're just short. I can't believe I let a shrimp like you...bully me into all this work."

Though he was breathless, Jeff's silver-gray eyes shone with a good humor that quickly faded as he searched her face. His gaze, stormy and intent, seemed to ask an unvoiced question. But his expression was so enigmatic that it left Hope at a loss for an answer.

"What?" she asked finally when he continued to stare at her.

He gave her a sad little smile before looking at Curt. "I've about had it."

"I know. Did you get dizzy this time?"

Jeff shook his head, sweat dripping from his collar-length hair.

"Good," Curt said, moving closer to his patient. "Let the braces hold you for just a second. Ease up on your grip. We're trying for balance here."

Hope watched Jeff concentrate as if trying to remember something he'd forgotten. The sweat ran in rivulets down his cheeks. He carefully eased some of the tension out of the muscles of his arms. A grin broke across his face but then he swayed a little. Curt was there just as Jeff's grip tightened on the bars.

"You did good," Curt said. "Before you know it you'll remember how to keep balanced. Now let's get you back in the chair."

"Oh!" Emily cried from the doorway. "Jeffrey, you bad boy. Keeping a secret like this. I didn't spank you enough. That's all there is to it. Breakfast is ready," she said finally, then a sob broke from her throat and she turned and scurried away.

"I'd better see to her. She loves you so much, Jeff.

I hope you realize that,'' Hope told him, and ran after Emily.

"Hope,'' Jeff said when he found her on the stone breakfast terrace several minutes later. "You didn't act the way I thought you would. You looked more afraid than happy.''

She shrugged. "Of course I was happy. I was worried. That's all. You're already all banged up. You said you fell on your first attempt. You're safe in the chair. You could get hurt worse than you are now.''

"Or I could learn how to put one foot in front of the other again.''

Hope smiled and took his hand. As always, a tiny thrill went through him at her touch. "That'll be great. You will. I know it. How tired are you from all that new activity?''

"Only a little. Why?''

"Because I wanted to bring Ruby over today, but she's a nightmare to trailer. I wondered if you'd do me a favor. Would you drive me over to Laurel Glen so I can ride her back? That way I can toss her blanket and some other equipment in the back of the van and not have to trailer her.''

Jeff wished she'd put this off a few days. He wondered if it was too soon after his talk yesterday with her father. Had Ross had enough time to think?

"I don't know, Hope,'' Jeff said, stalling. He hoped to put her off at least a few days. "Maybe that's not such a good idea.''

"I know it might be awkward for you, but you

could stay in the van. We'd be in and out inside of half an hour. I doubt my father will even see you.''

"Well, all right,'' he agreed hesitantly, thinking he should call ahead and warn Ross that the timetable had been moved up.

"Thanks. And will you make sure I don't forget to get my address book? I've gone so far as writing myself a note on my hand and I still forget to get it every time I go over there!''

Jeff nodded, thinking how odd it would be for Hope to have moved all of her stuff out of Laurel House. He couldn't imagine Laurel Glen without Hope. It had surprised him that Ross thought she should go elsewhere.

"Things aren't very good at Laurel Glen right now,'' Ross had said yesterday. Were tensions that high between Cole and his father? It was the only explanation. And all the more reason Hope and her father needed to patch things up. Even Meg Taggert had had enough and had left to take a cruise "to soothe her shattered nerves.'' Of course, Hope thought her aunt was trying to force the two men to deal with each other even if was only to say pass the salt at the dinner table.

Three hours later Jeff got himself situated behind the wheel of the van as Hope climbed in beside him. He could feel the tension coming off her in waves. "Hope, this is your home we're heading to. Has it been that bad when you've stopped by?''

Hope shrugged. "I'm worried about you and Dad. I don't want him to hurt you if he sees us."

"He won't hurt me. I promise you. The only reason I hesitated when you asked me to drive was that I still think you should be moving home."

"I'm twenty-seven years old. It's time I moved out on my own."

"You may be right about that but I hate to see you do it with this rift between you and Ross. That's the only part of this I object to. It isn't my place to object in the first place, though. It's just that Cole left with things unsettled between them and not only has their relationship gotten worse but Cole has real problems because of it."

Hope smiled. "I promise to work on it. Okay?"

Jeff nodded and took her hand where it lay fisted in her lap. "There's my little peacemaker," he teased and started the van.

As they reached the border of the two farms, the white vinyl fencing he'd had installed earlier in the year ended, and traditional whitewashed, wooden fencing began, signaling the change of ownership. Otherwise all else remained the same. Hills continued to roll one into the next, and sleek horses trotted across the green fields and tossed their heads, looking majestic and regal with shining manes and tails flowing in their wake.

As they drove under the wrought iron archway at Laurel Glen's main entrance, Jeff fought the urge to stop to admire the artistry of a bygone era. He'd always loved the spectacular archway with its graceful renderings of the state flower that gave Laurel Glen its name. The artisan had made the laurel appear as if it twined its way through a network of delicate iron latticework. Rarely was this one site left out of a pictorial done of the county. Especially now with the pink and white mountain laurel, still partially in bloom, bordering the drive on both sides.

Once the wealthiest farm in the area, Laurel Glen had nearly gone into bankruptcy because of estate taxes after Ross's father died. In his early twenties at the time, with two small children to support, Ross Taggert had fought to hold hearth and home together while rebuilding Laurel Glen's reputation and fortune from nearly the ground up. It was now the top horse farm in the tristate area, and it was all due to Hope's father.

And the man deserved the chance to repair his relationship with his daughter. While Addison Carrington had never earned Jeff's respect because of his shallow values, Ross had. His entire life whenever Jeff had to make a hard decision, he'd asked himself one question—what would Ross Taggert do?

If Jeff had one regret, it was that Addison had seen Jeff's feelings for Ross and had apparently set out to destroy any relationship the two had ever and would ever have.

The van topped a rise that hid all but the main house from view of the road. Laid out before them was the heart of Laurel Glen. On this farm, unlike his own, the barn and low stables fanned out before the house. They were nestled in the valley between the hill they'd just crested and an even higher rise where Laurel House sat. The stone facade of Laurel House rose from that farther mound like an elegant outcropping of nature. It seemed to keep guard over what it held most dear.

Four pristine brick and stone stable buildings formed an X with a competition-size ring at their apex. The original historical stone barn sat off to the left, in a clear position of honor. And from that precious cluster of buildings ran the fences, pastures and trails that completed all that was Laurel Glen.

He couldn't let Hope lose this.

Jeff pulled in next to the stable Hope indicated and set the parking brake. No sooner had he turned off the engine than the stable door opened and Ross and Cole stepped into the midday sunshine. Hope let out an agonized groan.

"Hey, don't assume the worst," Jeff admonished, watching the two men round the front of the van. Cole got to Hope's door first, and she put the window down. Ross stood behind his son, hanging back and looking as uncertain as Hope did.

Help me repair it, Lord, Jeff prayed.

"Hi, kitten. What brings you here?" Cole asked, though he knew, because Jeff had called and warned him of their visit.

"I...uh...I came to get Ruby," Hope stammered. "I thought I'd get more chance to ride her...you know...if she was at Lavender Hill."

Ross nodded. "Probably."

"We were just headed to the house," Cole said.

Ross pulled at the back of his neck as if the muscles were suddenly tight. "Uh...you two have lunch yet?" he asked.

"No," Jeff replied quickly before Hope could make excuses to shorten her visit. If this was an overture, he wasn't about to pass it up. Then a thought struck him. The main house sat high, surrounded by stone terraces that fell away down the hill in a series of three sets of stone stairs. He couldn't think of a way to get himself inside that didn't include someone dragging his chair up those graceful but numerous steps.

He felt suddenly like a wounded knight staring at an impenetrable castle and wondered if Ross had invited them knowing Jeff would be excluded by virtue of the layout of the house.

Hope was way ahead of him, though, and it was clear from her tone that she thought exactly that. "Laurel House isn't exactly handicap friendly, Dad." She all but growled the words.

"It's okay, Hope." Jeff jumped in. He was not going to let her throw away this overture for his sake—not again. "You can toss the equipment you were going to pick up in the van now and ride home on Ruby after your lunch settles a little. I'm sure Mrs. R will have something ready anyway."

"Dad already figured out how to get you inside," Cole said. "Drive around the side of the house and into the garage. There are only three steps into the house from there, and if the two of us can't hustle you in that way we're ready for a rest home."

Cole opened Hope's door and turned to Ross. "It's all settled. They're staying. Walk with Dad, kitten," he said as he handily slipped Hope from the car. "I'll get the garage door for Jeff. We'll see you two in there."

Hope looked at him, and Jeff nearly laughed at the deer-in-the-spotlight look on her face. She stepped away from the door, and Cole climbed in.

"So, old son," Cole said with a grin as he slammed the door and slouched in the seat. "You think my father has finally slipped a cog or what?"

Jeff laughed and started the van. In minutes he was pulling into the garage, then Cole hauled him backward up the three steps that led to a mudroom off the kitchen. If Ross had slipped a cog, Jeff hoped it stayed out of sync. Because Hope's father had looked very much like a tongue-tied male trying to find a way to apologize while maintaining his pride. Jeff knew the look. He'd been wearing it often enough of late.

Chapter Sixteen

Hope and Ross had a pleasant stroll up to the house, but she was aware of a certain restraint between them as if each feared treading on dangerous territory. Her father talked a bit about Laurel Glen's business and his upcoming search for a new trainer. Hope offered to fill in as much as possible and help with interviews and such whenever her duties at Lavender Hill allowed. Ross accepted with alacrity, though he didn't ask how much time she could give him.

They walked into Laurel House's sunny breakfast room just as Cole pushed Jeff in from the kitchen. Hope felt Ross tense next to her.

"I could have helped," he said, and Hope nearly cringed at his sharp tone. She said a quick prayer that he and Cole could get through at least one meal with a little peace between them. Their arguments were like a malignant force that seemed to infect everyone present, drawing bystanders into the fray with incredible efficiency. She'd seen it time and time again from the day after her mother was buried to the day she'd left Laurel Glen only weeks ago.

"No need," Cole said lightly. Hope was taken aback by the determination she saw in her brother's deep brown eyes. For her sake and Jeff's he didn't intend to let himself be baited. If only he could find that kind of restraint for himself and their father, she thought sadly. "Jeff's so good with this chair he nearly did all the work himself," Cole continued, boosting Jeff's chin up and examining his bruised face with all the concern of a dedicated healer. "I did wonder if you needed seat belts, though, bud. What did you do? Fall out on your head?"

"He fell trying to stand," Hope said, proud of Jeff's determination.

As he playfully batted Cole's hand away, Jeff shot them all a self-deprecating grin. "It wasn't supposed to turn out the way it did."

"Was that wise?" her father asked. The real concern in his voice had Hope staring in awe at the father she thought she knew.

Jeff shrugged. "They say you've got to crawl before you walk, but what you really have to be able to do is stand. I won't take a first step sitting in my chair."

Cole shook his head and took a seat at the table. "Well, be careful. If you need two people to spot for you, I'll run by and help Curt out. Just name the time."

"That's a great idea," Hope said. "Manny helped

this morning, but it occurred to me that if Jeff fell backward, he'd squash the poor little guy flat.''

"Consider me drafted then. That wouldn't be good for either of you. You need all the help around there you can get if you're going to get this idea of yours up and running.''

"So how *are* the plans coming along for the training facility?'' Ross asked, sitting next to Cole and reaching for the pitcher of iced tea in the middle of the table. "You talk to the Olympic committee yet?''

Jeff outlined what they'd done so far and explained that they probably wouldn't get the facility up and running for nine months to a year. There was a lot more red tape than they'd originally thought and so many other arrangements that had to be made that they'd decided not to rush. Jeff had also decided that he wanted the school to have a strong Christian influence. Both Cole and her father looked bewildered by what that meant.

"And the house needs work, too,'' Hope told them. "It'll house twenty kids easily with two in each room. Since each bedroom has a bath, that's one thing we don't have to worry about as far as renovations. But the marble has to go and the dining room has to be enlarged.''

"But, Jeff, your mother loved that marble,'' Ross teased.

"And, Hope, you always said it looks like an upscale hotel lobby,'' Cole added, pointing a teasing finger at her.

She felt a blush heat her face, and Jeff's deep chuckle sent shivers up Hope's spine.

"My sentiments exactly. We want the kids to feel at home. Not like they're at a hotel," Jeff joked.

The teasing and camaraderie transported Hope to another time, back to when Jeff ate nearly every other meal at Laurel Glen. Back before the accident that killed her mother. Before her father and brother couldn't be in the same room and not snipe at each other. Back when Jeff would ask her father about things his own father should have been available to answer for his son.

Once again conversation flowed, and the old pattern of teasing picked up nearly where it had left off the day before Cole was sent away. It wasn't as relaxed as it had been the day before their mother died and Cole had become increasingly hostile and angry, but it felt right for the first time in years. She didn't even mind that she was the brunt of her brother's witty tongue because, as always, Jeff was there to take the sting out of any mocking remark Cole could make.

She glanced at her father and noticed he looked angry but also that he had a faraway look in his eyes. She reached over and covered his hand with hers, hoping to pour oil on troubled waters while Jeff and Cole laughed and relived some wild escapade they'd all shared.

Ross's vision cleared. "Jeff," he said when a moment of silence gave him an opening. "Were you with Cole the night he stole the police car?"

All the good feelings in the room evaporated in an instant. "Dad," Cole snapped, his face cold and rigid. He was clearly about to continue when Jeff held his hand up and stopped him.

"It's all right. No. I wasn't with him. Cole did come over that night, but Mother sent him away. I had an appointment with my Calc tutor that she wouldn't let me put it off."

"I told you I wasn't with Jeff," Cole said, his teeth all but bared.

"Well, you were with someone. Chief Johnson saw someone running away. You would never say who it was."

"But I did tell you it wasn't Jeff."

Ross nodded. "I know. But Addison told me it was. At least he strongly implied that you were there," Ross explained, directing his comment to Jeff. "He apologized for not having the guts to turn you in. He begged me to understand all you'd lose if I said anything. Because you weren't a minor, you would have been instantly charged with a felony. I was furious but I didn't want that for you, either. If you weren't there why would he say you were?"

Cole looked utterly shocked but Jeff, while clearly shaken, nodded. His voice when he spoke, however, held a touch of bitterness. "I take it Addison had quite a lot to say to you about me over the years. I think I finally figured out why. He was jealous of you and my feelings for you. I can only guess, of course, but I think he set out to destroy our relationship. He hated that I respected you and all you stood for. Heritage meant nothing to him. He thought you were a fool to work so hard at building up the farm when you could have sold the land to a developer for millions. And he hated that I went to you for advice and took it.''

Her father looked physically ill. "You think he actually lied so I'd turn against you?"

"It's all I can come up with. He liked manipulating people."

"But he was—" Ross cut off what he'd been about to say and shook his head.

"My father," Jeff finished for him.

"Yeah…what can I say, Jeff? I've misjudged you for years. I guess I should have realized you couldn't change that much that quickly, but…" Everyone knew what he'd left unsaid. Cole had changed. Cole had changed overnight.

Jeff shrugged and spoke into the silence. Shaken and unmistakably sad, he said, "Addison was my father. Why would you doubt him? Why would anyone?"

"I'm so sorry. For the things I've said. For the way I acted when you got hurt. I don't know if you can understand what I felt. Here you were, the golden boy. Rolling in horse dung and coming up smelling like Chanel. You'd gotten an Ivy League degree and were headed for Olympic gold and I'd lost years with my son when we might have settled our differences. He got military school and you got college. I honestly thought that this time you'd been careless and had gotten what you deserved for a change. Then my daughter tells me to all but shove her position here and she runs off to play nursemaid. I've been furious and helpless to do anything with the anger. Every time I opened my mouth, I looked like a coldhearted so-and-so. If I had the man here right now I'd be tempted to throttle him. I believe he lied, but all this because he was jealous of me? You're sure?''

Jeff nodded. "Jealousy is the only thing I can come up with as an explanation for why he'd lie."

And indeed no one else could venture a different guess as to why Addison's version of that night should have been so different from Cole and Jeff's. Blessedly, the conversation veered off from there to talk of county politics then back to Jeff's training facility.

"I've been thinking, you two," Ross said. "You said you were going to be shut down during summers except for arranging for competitions for the scholarship students. Have you given any thought to changing your focus during those months? Maybe running day camps?"

Hope thought the idea was brilliant. "Jeff, that would solve your question about how to spot talent in underprivileged kids when they're not usually exposed to the equestrian world."

"Actually I was thinking of another kind of underprivileged kid," her father said. "Like the kids in the Special Olympics. Or the Sunshine camps. I understand handicapped kids really benefit from contact with horses. And I imagine Jeff could relate to handicapped kids the way no one else I know of who works with horses could. You'd be the perfect trainer for them even if you don't manage to get walking again. You could do a lot of good with this whole project, Jeff.''

"Dad, that's a great idea," Hope said, feeling her father had retracted his remark about Jeff being a worthless cripple.

Jeff was not as enthusiastic. He nodded, his thoughts clearly turned inward. "I'll give it some thought," he said and looked at her, his gaze riveted and riveting.

What are you thinking? she wondered, unable to look away. Did he understand her father's remark as a symbol of trust and value? She prayed he did, then caught sight of the clock.

"Good heavens, will you look at the time? What a bunch of chatterboxes we are. Listen, I'm going to go down to the stable and start getting things together. Jeff, why don't you follow with the van? I don't have much to load. I'll see you all in a few minutes.''

"Hope, there are some things of your mother's that I think it's time you have. And Cole, didn't you mention getting Jeff's opinion on that little filly you picked up last week? You kids go on ahead and leave the van here. I'll load the boxes up and bring the van down to stable four.''

Everyone agreed, but Hope wanted to run ahead and leave Cole and Jeff some time together. She noticed some of her men walking toward the stone barn. She wanted to be the one to tell them she wouldn't be returning except to fill in every once and a while, so she trotted after them.

"Tony. Maurice. Joseph!"

The men turned toward her, as did several others who stood around a pallet of hay they apparently intended to hoist into the loft. It wasn't the way she would have recommended doing it but guessed it could work to their advantage timewise.

"Listen up, guys. I wanted to let you all know I won't be back except to help out sometimes. I'm staying on at Lavender Hill as a partner and trainer of an Olympic facility Jeff wants to get up and running."

"Hey, way to go!" Maurice called.

At the same time Tony said, "Yeah, our loss is Carrington's gain."

Joseph, who rarely strung more than two words together in an hour, said, "We miss you already, boss lady."

A chorus of others added like sentiments, causing tears to dam up in Hope's throat. She was about to thank them all for their support when a strident voice echoed from inside the barn. "You lazy clowns want to stop flirting with the boss's daughter and get it in gear?"

"Uh-oh. Sorry, Ms. Taggert. Donovan's on the warpath again. The man's been a bear for months," Tony said. "Come on, boys. Let's give this crazy idea a try."

Hope stepped to the side and watched the men hoist the heavy load off the ground. For the life of her she didn't see how it was going to fit through the loft door, though. She walked forward, trying to get a better prospective.

Just as he and Cole made it to stable four, Jeff remembered he was supposed to remind Hope to get her address book. He left Cole and pushed himself toward where he saw Hope standing. She was laughing and talking with some men who were hoisting a pallet of hay. It looked like a bad way to handle so clumsy a load to him. He was sure it must be the angle he was at that made it look as if Hope was standing under the loft door, but his heart suddenly began to pound. He squinted against the glare of the sun, trying to see better. The height of the stack looked off, as if it was too tall to fit inside the opening. He pushed ahead faster.

Afraid for her, Jeff called Hope's name, but the men were all shouting as they pulled on the straining ropes. As he pumped his arms on the big rubber wheels, he looked up, and the top bale hit the header, causing the stack to list to one side.

"Hope!" he screamed, and she turned, surprise on her face. "The stack!" he yelled.

But she couldn't see what he saw from her vantage point, and rather than move, Hope look up in confusion, a frown creasing her brow.

A few feet from her, Jeff reached out to grab her as the pallet shifted above them and the bales tumbled free. Just as his hands gripped her arms and he pulled her to keep her from being crushed, Jeff felt the impact of a bale vibrate through Hope's body. She slumped forward into his arms.

The bales were tumbling amid the shouts of the men as they ran for cover. Jeff did the only thing he could think to do. He pulled her toward his chest and lurched out of the chair and over the side, causing it to overturn as they fell toward the ground. Bracing his arms around her like a safety cage, he hovered over Hope, protecting her beneath his body as the weight of the bales bore down on him.

Then it was over, and silence reigned.

"Jeff!" He heard Cole call from what sounded like a great distance. He was aware of the weight of several hundred pounds of hay on his shoulders and back. Thanks to all his exercise and probably gallons of adrenaline pumping through his veins, Jeff was able to stay on his forearms while the men pulled the bales off him. Fortunately, the overturned chair somehow kept the load off his legs.

Jeff blinked, trying to clear away the gritty hay dust and tears. Finally his vision cleared, and to his horror he saw that Hope lay still and pale beneath him.

"What nitwit thought this up?" Ross bellowed from above them. Jeff heard several voices answer at once as the men clamored to get through the hay to him and Hope.

It all seemed to be happening at a great distance, though, as Jeff's concentration remained fixed on Hope's motionless form. He could feel her shallow breathing but it did little to calm his thundering heart. He braced her head between his palms and talked to her, encouraging her to open her eyes, but she didn't respond.

One single horrifying thought paralyzed him as no fall from a horse ever could. What would he do if he lost her? He'd been facing a similar loss for months, but at least he'd have known she was alive though out of reach. And wouldn't that be a stupid waste? a quiet voice whispered.

"Are you all right?" Ross asked as the weight of the last bale was lifted off his back.

"It's Hope," Jeff said, not taking his eyes off her still features. "She's unconscious. A bale hit her before I could pull her out of the way. Somebody call nine-one-one."

Jeff saw his tears fall onto Hope's face and realized he was crying. But for the first time in his life he didn't care who saw his pain. What good was pride in an empty life? He'd been so absolutely stupid about everything. Suppose that bale injured her spine? What if she wound up like him? Would he love her less? Think less of her or need her inner strength and gentleness any less? Would *he* hesitate to marry *her* because she was physically limited? Of course, he wouldn't! Then why had he thought she should feel differently toward him?

Pride. He'd never let anyone see his pain. He'd presented facades to the world lest someone else find him wanting. Only with Hope and occasionally Cole had he shown his real self, and even then he'd hidden his most private feelings. He'd been a fool. Pride was an empty emotion full of self-pity and ultimately loneliness.

"Oh, please, dear God, don't let her be hurt!" he cried. Ross and Cole hunkered down next to them then. Cole reached over to check her pulse, and Ross put a hand on Jeff's back as if trying to brace him for bad news. "Don't take her from me," Jeff begged the Lord whom he'd known so short a time.

"Her pulse is fine," Cole assured him. "She's probably just taking a little snooze to scare us all."

"And there's an ambulance on the way. Let's get you back in your chair so Cole can take a better look at her," Ross suggested.

He knew her father was right, but he couldn't make himself move. Fear held him paralyzed more than his injured spine ever had. "I was so stupid," he sobbed, looking at Cole. "I told her we were only ever going to be friends. I didn't want to tie her to me while I was like this. Why was I so stupid?"

"Because you're a man and I'm told by my sister that we're all stupid," Cole explained patiently. "Now come on and let's get you up."

About to acquiesce, Jeff saw Hope's lashes flicker. "Hope, sweetheart, can you hear me?" he whispered, his throat tight with fear and raw with tears.

"Of course I can hear you. You're two inches from my ear," she muttered.

Jeff breathed a sigh of relief and, still holding her head between his hands, dropped his forehead onto hers for a long moment and closed his eyes in a quick prayer of gratitude.

Cole reacted to Hope's smart remark and snickered, dropping his head onto his arm where it was braced on the ground, his shoulders shaking in relieved laughter.

Ross chuckled, too, and smacked Jeff on the shoulder. "Come on, let's get you back in your chair before she slugs you for hovering. Hope hates it when people hover."

Jeff still couldn't let go of his precious burden, nor could he drag his gaze from hers. Instead he balanced his weight on one forearm and brushed some hay off her cheek. He tried to smile, afraid his somber mood might frighten her, but he couldn't get the sight of that tilting pallet out of his head. Of the bales tumbling. Of her standing so vulnerable beneath them.

He could have lost her so easily, and still might. He'd been so stubborn, telling himself it was okay to break her heart with a lie about his feelings for her because she was better off without him. He'd been wrong, and now he didn't know how she felt about him anymore.

He'd been so awful in those first days. Had she seen a side of him that had killed her love? Was she still at Lavender Hill because of guilt? Mere friendship? Or love?

Because of his pride, he didn't know.

But then Hope answered Ross's banter. "That depends on who's doing the hovering," she whispered and reached up to caress Jeff's cheek, a loving smile brightening her face.

Jeff leaned down and gave into the wants and needs

he'd denied for months. He cupped her cheek and brushed her lips with his once, twice, then he kissed her with all the love he felt in his heart.

Why had he fought this for so long? Where was the loss of pride in this? Where was the selfishness he feared would take over his soul if he took what she offered? This was all about beauty and need and desire. This was life at its most pure. This communion of spirit could be nothing less than a love sent by God.

Chapter Seventeen

Hope put her feet up on the sofa and stared at the lights of the main house. She thought over the day, hardly able to take it all in. It had started with Jeff and his incredible surprise in the exercise room and had ended with him kissing her, as Cole said, "Before God and everyone."

Then the paramedics had arrived, and she hadn't spoken to Jeff again. After checking both of them over for injuries, the technicians had decided they should both be taken to the E.R. because she had lost consciousness and because of Jeff's previous serious back injury.

It was a precaution, they had assured Jeff, and his protests to the contrary that he was fine, they had insisted on transporting both of them. Her last glimpse of him being strapped onto a backboard and loaded into an ambulance felt frighteningly like a rerun rather than a simple case of déjà vu.

That was the last time she'd seen him. Cole had brought her home, relaying the message that Jeff's shoulders and back were badly bruised but so far nothing else had turned up. Though he'd apparently protested that he had suffered no other ill effects from his heroic actions, they'd still insisted he wait till his neurologist could see him. Dr. Chin had arrived and decided that to be on the safe side he'd like to do a CAT scan, so Jeff and her father were still at the hospital.

It frightened her to think of Jeff putting himself between her and hundreds of pounds of falling hay bales. He could so easily have been injured all over again. And it would have been her fault for wandering where she hadn't belonged.

She closed her eyes and lay her aching head back, listening to Cole rattle around in her kitchen. She had only a slight concussion, but Cole wouldn't go home. She wanted him to. Desperately. When Jeff got home, she didn't want her sardonic brother there teasing him about that kiss. It had been too special to make light of.

That kiss had been a moment out of time that she would revisit and cherish to her dying day. She'd awakened to Cole's voice, then Jeff's had come from a mere inches away. She'd thrown the wisecrack back in answer to his question before she'd identified what it was about his voice that sounded odd. She'd forced her eyes open then, her concern for Jeff overriding her foggy state. It had been an utter shock to have the tears she'd thought she heard in his voice confirmed.

Jeff had breathed a deep sigh then and dropped his forehead onto hers, his eyes closed. He'd held her so gently. So protectively. Then Cole and her father tried to get him to let her go. He'd pulled back a little but then his gaze caught on hers and held them both suspended in a place and time of their own for long moments. She'd watched in fascination as he'd battled some inner demon while her father and brother tried to lighten the moment with teasing banter. Nervous suddenly about what was going on inside Jeff's head, she'd chimed in, too. In doing so, however, she'd given away her feelings for Jeff to anyone who'd cared to listen.

And Jeff had apparently listened, responding to her confession in a surprisingly wonderful way. He'd kissed her. And what a kiss it had been! Hope no longer doubted his love but she had no idea what he planned to do about it. It was like his effort at standing that morning. A first step on a new branch of a long road with no guarantee that he'd ever make it to that ephemeral final destination.

Cole preached cautious optimism, and she agreed in principle. A simple kiss couldn't be as monumental as it felt to her. Jeff had probably kissed hundreds of women. But for some reason Hope was still elated out of all proportion or sense.

And she wanted to see him. She wanted to find out if that kiss had been one in a million or just one of hundreds. If it had meant as much to him as it had to her. If it had opened the floodgates to the affection and chemistry she'd felt flow from him to her the night of the Valentine's dance party and that day before his accident.

Memories of those hours had sustained her all these lonely months, and now she had one more memory to tuck away for her dreams.

Cole tiptoed into the quaint little parlor and stood watching his little sister sleep the sleep of the innocent. Jeff was a lucky man. Cole hoped that kiss meant Jeff was ready to reach out and grab the brass ring. Women like his sister didn't come into a man's life every day.

In fact, Cole was nearly sure women like Hope were an endangered species. Though he hoped he'd be smart enough to run the other way if he ever ran across one, Jeff had better not try it. The truth was that Cole didn't even really know who *he* was, so there was no way he could commit himself to another person. But Jeff Carrington had better be good and ready, because slugging a man in a wheelchair was going to go against one of Cole's basic rules of life. If, however, Jeff had raised Hope's expectations only to send her into crash-and-burn mode, as her brother, that was exactly what he intended to do to his best friend.

Cole turned as the front door opened and his father came quietly in. His stomach instinctively tightened.

"How is she?" Ross whispered.

"A little headachy. I gave her something for it." At his father's sharp look Cole gritted his teeth. "Acetaminophen, Dad. I know she isn't a horse."

A look of chagrin crossed his father's face, which was progress, in a way. "Sorry. Jeff checked out fine. He'll be doing therapy in technicolor for a while but, considering the alternative, I'm mighty grateful he put himself in harm's way. You think it's okay to leave her alone?"

Cole nodded, trying not to show his surprise that Ross had actually solicited his medical opinion. "They said her concussion was extremely mild, so yeah. I asked Curt to stop and check on her every once in a while tonight."

Ross nodded and stared at Hope. "So you think I'm going to have to punch out Carrington or is he going to come up to scratch?"

Cole chuckled and opened the door, reveling in the moment of camaraderie. "You'll have to stand in line if he doesn't. He may be tough to catch, though. I'll bet he had that chair going twenty-five miles an hour this afternoon."

Jeff watched Cole and Ross drive past on their way home. He swung the chair away from the window and rolled across the hardwood floor to the mirrors, then wheeled away and back to the window. He stopped in the middle of the room on the fourth pass and chuckled. Pacing was certainly easier in a chair.

He should just go to her, tell her he loved her and ask her to marry him. But he'd promised both Cole and Ross that, unless he could walk, he wouldn't tell her how he felt. Of course, now he knew he'd been wrong and they hadn't asked for his promise in the first place. In fact, unless he'd misread Ross, he was going to be pretty annoyed if there wasn't a wedding in the offing. And soon.

So what was holding him back? He'd admitted to himself it had been pride that had held him back till now. Jim Dillon had been right. Hope didn't need physical strength in a husband. Jeff was still the same man he'd been before his accident and before he saved her this afternoon. He was still physically limited. He still wanted her.

But does she still want you? What if you misread her response to Cole? Her smile? Her part in that kiss?

Jeff heard the questions and knew immediately what the tightening in his gut meant. He was afraid she felt only pity for him. No. He was afraid he'd killed her love months ago acting like such a jerk. But if he let that fear stop him, what was really stopping him was his pride again.

His mind made up, Jeff showered, dressed in khakis and a sports shirt then headed to his office. It took some doing to pull himself up so he could open the safe, but he was determined to do at least this on his own. It wasn't pride, though. He just didn't want anyone else to know before Hope what he intended.

He made a grab for the jewel case and dropped backward into his chair when his hand closed around the velvet box. Heart pounding, he let out a tired but elated breath. Then he opened the box he'd stuffed in the safe years ago after his parents' funerals. He rooted through the gold and platinum, bypassed a string of pearls, a sapphire and diamond tennis brace- let and ignored scores of other high-priced baubles that his mother had favored. He was looking for his grandmother's engagement ring, a simple one-carat solitaire that had been in his family for generations.

He found it, and a helpless smile tugged at the cor- ners of his mouth. It was perfect for Hope. Simple. Delicate. Elegant. Now if she would only accept it. And him.

He was halfway through the house when it struck him that his stomach was jumpy with nerves. It re- minded him of his first date. He smiled, unable to remember the face of that long-ago young girl. The only face he could recall at that moment was Hope's.

His stomach did a flip, and he remembered another date—another day he'd been nervous. He'd been headed over to go riding with Hope—the ride that had shattered his world. *Please, Lord, let this turn out better than that date.*

Date!

He'd never even taken her on a real date. The brunch at the Dupont had started out as one but he'd turned it into a business luncheon by asking her to be his partner, so Jeff figured it didn't count. Here he was about to ask Hope to marry him and he'd never even taken her on a date.

Jeff looked at the ring. It couldn't wait. He couldn't wait. *He* grinned. Today was June third. If she agreed to marry him, he'd take her on an official date every June third for the rest of their lives to make up for the oversight.

Just let her say yes, Lord. I don't want to live without her.

He was at the door to the homestead house in minutes, the ring on his pinky and a bunch of flowers he'd swiped off the breakfast room table in his lap. The lights were on in the parlor, and he could see Hope curled up and asleep on the sofa. He turned away, disappointed. He hated the idea of waking her. Halfway back to the house, he stopped.

This couldn't wait. He turned back.

"Wake up, sleepyhead," he called through the open window before he could change his mind.

Hope sat up like a bolt of lightning had struck nearby and looked around, confused.

"I'm outside," he told her. "Are you up to coming out here so we can talk? It's a nice night. We could sit in the rose arbor."

Hope agreed and arrived not long after he did. She'd changed into a soft peach-colored lounging set that wasn't quite pajamas and not street wear, either. She looked like peaches and cream and good enough to eat in the low exterior lighting. Jeff swallowed— hard.

"It's a pretty night," she remarked as she drew nearer.

"Not half as pretty as you. These are for you." He handed her the flowers, the stems wrapped in paper towel. "How's your head?"

Hope looked at the flowers, puzzled. "Thanks. My head's fine." She smiled. "How's my hero?"

He grinned at that appellation then sobered. "Nervous," he said truthfully.

Hope sat heavily on the stone bench. Clearly alarmed, she reached for his hand. "The CAT scan showed more damage?" she cried.

Jeff shook his head and took her hand in his, fighting the urge to yank her into his arms. "My back's fine," he said. "It's my heart."

"Your heart!" she yelped.

Fighting a grin, he nodded solemnly. "Uh-huh. I lost it. It happened months ago, but I lied so no one would find out. So *you* wouldn't find out. I can't hide it anymore, though." He could almost see the truth dawn on her sweet features.

"You can't?"

"Nope." His heart contracted at the longing in her eyes. He couldn't draw this out any further. "I love you, Hope."

"You love me?"

"With all my heart. And I don't want you to leave. Not permanently, anyway. Just till after the wedding."

Beginning to regain her composure, Hope raised that adorable imperious eyebrow. "Wedding?"

Jeff pulled the ring off his pinky. "Will you marry me, sweetheart? Will you come be my love as well as my partner?"

Hope was tempted to pinch herself. Could she still be in the homestead house, asleep, dreaming her heart's desire? She looked around the flagstone garden and at the latticework archways of the rose arbor that surrounded them. She felt the stone bench beneath her. The cool late spring air. This definitely didn't feel like a dream. Jeff was sitting there looking hopeful with the most compelling look in his eyes.

"You love me?" she asked, checking her facts. "You want to marry me?"

"If you love me. And if you'll have me. Is that so hard to believe?"

"You said I was like a sister to you."

Even in the low light of the garden lanterns, Hope could see his silvery eyes glitter. "I'd get arrested in nearly every civilized country in the world for feeling this way about a sister."

Still holding her hand, he pulled her to her feet and into his lap. Then he kissed each of her fingers, holding her gaze captive. Warmth spread through her from her fingers to her toes.

"I thought for a long time I was hiding my feelings for your sake. But today, you could have been hurt as badly or worse than I was in February, and I'd still have loved you. Why did I think your feelings should work any differently? Because I'm supposed to be this big strong guy? I told myself when I walked—if I walked—then I'd tell you how I feel. Today I realized that was my pride talking. And I was wrong. I could have lost you today and I'd never have told you how I feel. I do love you, Hope."

"And I love you," she said simply. Finally.

A smile brightened Jeff's eyes, though his mouth remained solemn. "Will you marry me, Hope? Will you make me the happiest, luckiest guy in the world?'' He pulled a pretty, old-fashioned diamond solitaire off his finger and held it out for her to accept.

Funny, she thought, looking down on his golden head as he slid the ring on her finger. He'd been the one seeking the gold and she'd been the one to win it in the end.

Epilogue

Ross jumped from the family's carefully preserved antique open carriage. Thanks to a cool sunny day he'd been able to bring Hope to the church the way every Taggert bride had arrived at her wedding for the last hundred and fifty years. Hope had insisted on it.

She'd always been a funny kid, clinging to some traditions while busting others wide open. So today his horse-training daughter planned to marry the boy next door in a church that used to be a barn while wearing her grandmother's veil and the latest in wedding dresses.

And she was a vision in the simple sleeveless dress his sister had said was made of something called tissue taffeta. The yards of material were gathered at her waist to form a full skirt, and made her look like the princess he'd always considered her.

Ross tied the horses to an ornamental piece of split

rail fence, then went to escort his princess to meet her prince. He squinted as he looked up. The midsummer sun and the bright white dress combined to temporarily blind him. "You're beautiful, princess," he said and lifted her to the ground. She weighed less than a feather, but mistaking her delicate stature for fragility was a mistake he didn't make anymore. That error had gotten him in more hot water over the years than he cared to think about on such a happy day.

"You haven't called me that in years," she said, looking at him with her deep blue eyes shining with happiness.

Ross chuckled. "I was afraid of having my head handed to me."

"Was I that bad?"

"No worse than I was," he admitted. "It's hard for a father to let go and stop trying to protect his little girl." He hesitated. "Hope, if you ever need anything, remember I'm here."

Hope reached up and put her hand on his shoulder. "We'll be just fine. I know you worry because he's still in a chair—"

"No, that's not it. It's just that it seems like yesterday that your mother and I brought a fragile little bundle of nothing home and called her Hope Taggert. Now it feels like I blinked my eyes and she's about to change her name. It's a lot for a father to take in. But if you have to take another name, I'm glad it's Jeff's. He's a good man. I just wish I hadn't been so stubborn about him all these years. I let Addison's lies cheat us out of a lot of good years."

"Well, we have lots of years ahead to make up lost time."

"Time!" he all but yelped, checking his watch. "We'd better stop yammering and get you in there before your groom paces all the rubber off his wheels."

Jim Dillon greeted them at the door. Ross's problems with God always made him a little uncomfortable with the easygoing preacher, but today it was tough to resist the younger man's congenial smile.

"Oh, good. You're here," Dillon said, offering Ross his hand. "Give me a minute to get down front. I'll signal Holly to start playing the wedding march, then you two come on ahead. Meg and Cole are down there already, the way we decided last night."

"Okay. Good to go," Ross said then turned to Hope. "Ready to become a Carrington?"

Her happy smile lit his heart. "More than ready."

The first strains of the wedding march floated to the back of the sanctuary. "Good thing, 'cause we're on."

Jeff's two ushers, Curt Madden—tall, muscular and blond—and Manny Hernandez—short, slight and dark—opened the doors. With his eyes, Ross traced the white runner down the length of the aisle to the raised platform. On it sat a flower-bedecked replica of the Laurel Glen entrance archway. Jeff had commissioned it for the wedding as a symbol that Hope might be taking *his* name but he was joining *her* family.

Ross looked to the right and saw something he

knew Hope from her lower vantage point could not. Jeff wasn't sitting in his wheelchair. Ross could see the top of his blond head peeking over the crowd. He couldn't imagine how desperately Jeff must have wanted to greet Hope at the altar standing on his own two feet if he was willing to risk this. The braces that allowed him to stand were heavy and uncomfortable, and there was always the risk of falling.

Ross started them walking toward the man who was his only daughter's future, then he squeezed Hope's hand and leaned sideways a bit to whisper, "Jeff's standing, princess."

"I thought he might try something like this," she whispered back. "He's been working almost nonstop at his therapy."

When they got about three-quarters of the way down the aisle the congregation suddenly sat, giving them a complete view of Jeff.

And a wonderful gift.

He stood straight and tall, no wheelchair, braces or walker in sight. Hope gasped then let out a little squeak of a sob. Jeff held out his hand and walked forward a few steps as if he'd been born on those two feet and sturdy legs.

Ross let go of Hope when she strained forward. "Go ahead, princess," he whispered, "there's your future standing there on his own two feet."

Hope looked at him, tears making her sapphire eyes glitter. Then she turned and walked forward toward a golden future....

*   *   *   *   *

Dear Reader,

I hope you've enjoyed the first book of my new LAUREL GLEN series and the updates on the congregation at the Tabernacle.

Hope and Jeff's story came to me as I watched a film of a three-day event on television. Due to an injury in my twenties that prevented me from riding, I could relate to never again flying over trails with the wind in my hair. But it was only recreation for me. I could only imagine what it would be like to be at the top of the sport and lose the complete use of my legs.

And so Jeff, the golden boy of the equestrian world, was born—fully grown. What would he do without God to give him strength? He'd need someone who loved him already, since he would, no doubt, be angry and not very lovable. She'd need to be caring but strong. And she'd need to be well centered in the Lord so she could show him what he really needed in his life. And so Hope, voice of Jeff's conscience, came to be.

Sometimes the Lord just has to knock out all the props to get us to listen to Him and His plan for our lives. Jeff finally listened and found in that golden moment that he didn't have to be alone ever again because he had a Father watching over him. In books two and three of LAUREL GLEN, Hope's father and brother will both learn the same lesson and then some.

I love hearing from my readers and can be reached at c/o VFRW, P.O. Box 350, Wayne, PA 19087-0350.

Sincerely,

Kate Welsh

Next Month From Steeple Hill's

Love Inspired®

JUDGING SARA

by *Cynthia Rutledge*

When there are threats on Sara Michaels's life, the beautiful Christian singer reluctantly accepts the protection of her gruff, hard-to-please bodyguard. The two share an immediate attraction, but they couldn't be more different! Can this unexpected love survive a shocking deception?

Don't miss
JUDGING SARA
On sale December 2001

Next Month
From Steeple Hill's

Love Inspired

A GROOM WORTH WAITING FOR

by *Crystal Stovall*

Jilted at the altar by her fiancé, Amy Jenkins vows to start a new life in Lexington, Kentucky. But her plans go terribly awry when she's held up in a convenience store robbery! Having survived the attack thanks to a dynamic stranger, she finds herself drawn deeply into Matthew Wynn's life. Does God's plan for her future include finding in Matthew a groom worth waiting for?

Don't miss
A GROOM WORTH WAITING FOR
On sale November 2001

Next Month From Steeple Hill's

Love Inspired

LOVE ONE ANOTHER

by *Valerie Hansen*

Romance blooms when Zac Frazier and his little boy move into Tina Braddock's quaint neighborhood. Although the compassionate day-care worker knows the pitfalls of letting anyone get too close, she can't resist extending a helping hand to the dashing single dad and his adorable son. But a heavy-hearted Tina fears that their blossoming relationship will wilt if her shameful secret is ever exposed. Turning to the good Lord for support, Tina can only pray for the inner strength she desperately needs to trust in the power of love....

Don't miss
LOVE ONE ANOTHER
On sale November 2001

Next Month
From Steeple Hill's

Love Inspired

A BUNGALOW FOR TWO

by *Carole Gift Page*

Book #3 in
THE MINISTER'S DAUGHTER
miniseries

To escape her troubles, Frannie Rowlands finds sanctuary in an oceanside bungalow and becomes inexplicably drawn to her mysterious neighbor after he heroically comes to her rescue. Can their faith in God—and in each other—help them pave a loving future together?

Don't miss
A BUNAGLOW FOR TWO
On sale December 2001

Love Inspired